## Devil may care . . .

"Jackson!" Longarm said sharply, trying to get through to the man. "Jackson, wake up!"

Jackson tried to focus bleary, pain-filled eyes on the man who knelt beside him.

"Who paid you to bushwack me? Where's Angela Boothe?"

Jackson opened his mouth, but all that came out was a thin cry of pain as shattered bone grated together in his jaw. Longarm grabbed his chin, which made Jackson whimper even harder, and jammed the barrel of the Colt into the soft hollow of his throat.

"I'm gonna let go of you in a minute," Longarm said, "and then you're gonna tell me what I want to know. If you don't, I'll make you hurt so much you'll beg me to pull the trigger and send a bullet up through your brain. You got that, Jackson?"

Longarm let go of Jackson's jaw but kept the gun on him. Jackson struggled to form coherent words. "Stock . . ." he managed. "Stock . . . man . . ."

"You mean a rancher?" Longarm asked.

"Try . . . dent . . . try . . ."

"Try to dent what? Damn it, make sense!"

"Gone," Jackson mumbled. "Gone . . . to the devil . . ."

Suddenly, his back arched, his eyes opened wide, and a soundless scream came out of his mouth. He slumped down, a final breath rattling in his throat . . .

**TABOR EVANS**

# LONGARM

## AND THE DEVIL'S BRIDE

**J**

**JOVE BOOKS, NEW YORK**

**THE BERKLEY PUBLISHING GROUP**
**Published by the Penguin Group**
**Penguin Group (USA) Inc.**
**375 Hudson Street, New York, New York 10014, USA**
Penguin Group (Canada), 10 Alcorn Avenue, Toronto, Ontario M4V 3B2, Canada
(a division of Pearson Penguin Canada Inc.)
Penguin Books, Ltd. 80 Strand, London WC2R 0RL, England
Penguin Group Ireland, 25 St. Stephen's Green, Dublin 2, Ireland (a division of Penguin Books Ltd.)
Penguin Group (Australia), 250 Camberwell Road, Camberwell, Victoria 3124, Australia
(a division of Pearson Australia Group Pty. Ltd.)
Penguin Books India Pvt. Ltd., 11 Community Centre, Panchsheel Park, New Delhi—110 017, India
Penguin Group (NZ), Cnr. Airborne and Rosedale Roads, Albany, Auckland 1310, New Zealand
(a division of Pearson New Zealand Ltd.)
Penguin Books (South Africa) (Pty.) Ltd., 24 Sturdee Avenue, Rosebank, Johannesburg 2196, South
Africa

Penguin Books Ltd., Registered Offices: 80 Strand, London WC2R 0RL, England

This is a work of fiction. Names, characters, places, and incidents either are the product of the author's imagination or are used fictitiously, and any resemblance to actual persons, living or dead, business establishments, events, or locales is entirely coincidental.

LONGARM AND THE DEVIL'S BRIDE

A Jove Book / published by arrangement with the author

PRINTING HISTORY
Jove edition / October 2004

ISBN: 0-515-13836-3

JOVE®
Jove Books are published by The Berkley Publishing Group,
a division of Penguin Group (USA) Inc.
375 Hudson Street, New York, New York 10014.
JOVE is a registered trademark of Penguin Group (USA) Inc.
The "J" design is a trademark belonging to Penguin Group (USA) Inc.

PRINTED IN THE UNITED STATES OF AMERICA

10  9  8  7  6  5  4  3  2  1

# Chapter 1

Longarm had seen some strange things in the time he had packed a badge for Uncle Sam. He had tracked a Wendigo, dug up the bones of a critter the Indians called a Thunder Lizard, and crossed swords with what looked for all the world like the ghost of a long-dead pirate. He had gotten in a ruckus with a gent who wore the armor of an English knight, and another in the outfit of a Spanish conquistador. Bank robbers, counterfeiters, stagecoach thieves, diamond smugglers, cold-blooded murderers, and plain and simple lowlifes had all tried on numerous occasions to ventilate him.

But never—until tonight—had he seen a fella with the head of a goat, or a beautiful naked gal stretched out and tied down on an unholy altar of black stone.

And it would be all right with him if he never saw such things again.

It all started a couple of weeks earlier, on a beautiful spring morning in Denver, the sort of day that put a little extra bounce in Longarm's step and made him whistle a tune as he climbed the steps of the federal building on Colfax Avenue. The time was almost ten o'clock, which

1

meant he was nearly an hour late and Chief Marshal Billy Vail would probably chew on his ass because of it, but even that knowledge wasn't enough to dampen Longarm's mood. He had spent the night with a friendly widow woman he knew, and the pleasures they had shared left a warm memory in Longarm's brain.

He already had an unlit cheroot in his mouth when he walked into the outer office. Henry, the four-eyed young gent who played the typewriter for Vail, looked up with an unwholesome smile. Longarm and Henry had been carrying on a sort-of-friendly feud for several years, and if Henry was happy, it didn't bode well for the big deputy marshal.

"You were supposed to be here at nine," Henry said.

"That's true," Longarm replied mildly.

"Marshal Vail is upset with you."

Longarm rolled the cheroot to the other side of his mouth and said, "Hell, Billy's been riled at me a heap of times before. I'm still here, ain't I?"

"Yes, but this time he has an urgent wire from Washington that requires your attention. He sent a messenger to your place an hour ago, but you weren't there."

Longarm frowned. This *did* sound a little more serious than usual. Vail didn't often send someone to look for him. And of course, he hadn't been in his rented room on the other side of Cherry Creek. In fact, an hour earlier, he had still been in Joyce Madison's bed.

For that matter, he had still been in Joyce Madison. . . .

With a little shake of his head, Longarm put that memory out of his mind. "What's the telegram about, Henry?"

Henry sniffed. "I'll let Marshal Vail tell you."

"Fine," Longarm said as he started for the door of the inner office. "If you don't know—"

"I never said that! I know what's in the wire. I saw it."

"Well, then . . . ?"

Henry started to say something else but caught himself before he could. "Oh, no. You're not going to trick me, Deputy. You just go on in and talk to Marshal Vail. I'm sure he'll have *plenty* to say to you."

Longarm's teeth clenched on the cheroot. If that was the way Henry wanted to play it, that was fine. He rapped on the door, then grasped the knob and turned it as Vail bellowed, "Who the hell is it?"

"Just me, Billy," Longarm said as he stepped into the chief marshal's office. "Henry said you wanted to see me?"

Over the years of his service as a lawman, first as a Texas Ranger and then as chief marshal of this district for the U.S. Justice Department, Billy Vail had gained weight and lost hair until he looked more like some sort of pink-cheeked cherub than the hell-roaring star packer he had been . . . and still was, in his heart. He rode a desk these days, and he slapped a palm down on it with a sound almost like a gunshot.

"Long! Get in here!"

Longarm took the red leather chair in front of the desk and cocked his right ankle on his left knee. He reached into his vest pocket and fished out a lucifer to light his cheroot, but before he could snap the match to life on an iron-hard thumbnail, Vail said, "There's no time for that, damn it. Read this."

He shoved a yellow telegraph flimsy across the desk toward Longarm.

Longarm leaned forward and picked up the message. His keen eyes quickly scanned the words printed on it. He glanced up at Vail and said, "Lord and Lady Beechmuir?"

Vail grunted. "You remember *them,* I reckon?"

Longarm remembered John and Helena Boothe, all right. Awhile back the British couple, members of the nobility in that far-off country, had been involved in a case that had sent Longarm scurrying around the Brazos country down in Texas, looking for a legendary monster called the Brazos Devil. He had almost gotten killed a couple of times during that scrape, and though he didn't think of Lord and Lady Beechmuir very often, when he did it was not with great fondness. Helena, though beautiful, had been something of a bitch, in fact.

However, they seemed to have a higher opinion of him, because the telegram from the Justice Department stated that a request had been relayed to it from the State Department, a request that Deputy Marshal Custis Long be assigned to a sensitive case involving a foreign national visiting the United States, a young lady named Angela Boothe.

"Yeah, I remember them," Longarm said sourly in answer to Vail's question. His good mood had evaporated, and the swiftness with which it had vanished surprised even him. "Who's this Angela Boothe, their daughter?"

Longarm didn't recall any mention of Lord and Lady Beechmuir having a daughter, but of course it was possible.

Vail shook his head. "Your guess is as good as mine. You'll have to go to Kansas City and talk to a fella there from the State Department. He'll have all the details."

"So you *are* assigning me to this case?"

"Damn right I am," Vail snapped. "The State Department asked Justice for you, and Justice asked me, so you're going to Kansas City. I'm not sure why those Britishers want you in particular to handle this, unless it's because you kept them from getting killed down in Texas, but that's not my lookout." Vail leaned back in his chair and glared across the desk at Longarm. "Get your travel vouchers from Henry and make the eleven o'clock train."

Longarm glanced at the banjo clock on the wall. "That's less'n an hour from now, Billy," he pointed out.

"I can tell time! Now get going."

4

Vail might have mellowed some as he got older, but today he was as prickly as a cactus. Longarm knew it wouldn't do any good to argue with him or ask if he could take a later train. The chief marshal's mind was made up, and as a deputy, it was Longarm's job to follow orders. He tried to do that, at least most of the time . . . when it was reasonable and there wasn't a better way to do things.

He stood up. The visit had been so short he hadn't even removed the flat-crowned, snuff-brown Stetson from his head. He clenched his teeth on the cheroot and nodded. "I reckon I'll be met at the depot in Kansas City?"

"I'll wire the State Department fella that you're coming."

Henry had a smirk on his face when Longarm emerged from the inner office. "Been listening at the door, have you?" Longarm growled.

"I didn't have to listen. I told you, I know what's going on around here. Marshal Vail trusts me."

"You ain't the one he's sending to Kansas City."

"No, but I'd go if he asked me to, and without complaint, too."

"Just give me the travel vouchers."

Henry handed over the paperwork Longarm would need for his train trip. He would make the hop north to Cheyenne on the Denver & Rio Grande, then catch a Union Pacific eastbound to Kansas City. The trip would take most of a day, what with all the stops along the way. The train would pull into Kansas City early the next morning.

As usual, he would have to sleep sitting up, Longarm thought. It would make for a long, unpleasant night . . . a night he had planned to spend with the Widow Madison. He grimaced as he tucked the papers away inside his coat and left the federal building.

Since he had no real idea what this job was going to require, he just packed a small valise and didn't take his

Winchester and saddle. If he had to pick up more gear, he could do it later. He arrived at the Denver train station with time to spare and was settled in his seat in one of the D&RG coaches before the whistle sounded and the big Baldwin locomotive puffed out of the station. As the train began to rock along the rails, he took out the cheroot he hadn't had the chance to smoke earlier. He got it lit and drew the smoke deep in his lungs.

Longarm would have liked more details on this assignment, so that he would know what was waiting for him in Kansas City. But he was relatively certain of one thing:

Lord and Lady Beechmuir wouldn't have asked for him, special-like, if there wasn't a heap of trouble on the horizon.

# Chapter 2

The man who worked for the State Department was named Stewart Winchell. He was tall and well dressed and had blond hair and a pair of spectacles perched on his nose. He might have been fairly muscular if he'd ever had to do any work besides sitting at a desk. As things stood, though, he was soft, and the handshake he gave Longarm was limp.

Winchell had been waiting on the platform of the Union Pacific depot when the eastbound train rolled in. He must have been given Longarm's description, because as soon as Longarm stepped off the train, Winchell held up a hand and called, "Marshal! Marshal Long! Over here!"

Longarm's jaw tightened. The leather case containing his badge and bona fides was tucked away inside his coat, and there was nothing about him to announce that he was a star packer. So this dudish-looking fella had gone and done it for him. Longarm didn't know whether the case would require him to keep his identity a secret, but now it might be too late for that.

Longarm strode over, listened to the State Department man introduce himself, and then shook Winchell's dead fish of a hand. "I have a room for you at the Metrolite Hotel," Winchell said. "I'm staying there, too, so it'll make it more convenient for us to work together."

"Hold on a minute, old son," Longarm said. "You're getting carried away with that apple. Better eat it one bite at a time."

Winchell stared at him uncomprehendingly.

"Nobody ever said we were working together," Longarm explained. "The way I had it figured, you'd tell me whatever it is I need to know, and then I'll go on about my business, whatever that is."

"Oh." Winchell blinked blue eyes behind the spectacles. "You see, my superior, the undersecretary, instructed me to assist you in any way possible to bring this matter to a speedy, satisfactory conclusion, so naturally I assumed that would entail a certain amount of cooperation and mutual effort between us."

Longarm put a cheroot between his teeth and bit down hard on it. "Does this Metrolite Hotel have a dining room?"

"Why, yes, it does."

"Then let's go get some breakfast. I didn't eat on the train."

Longarm strode out of the station. Despite the fact that Winchell was almost as tall, the State Department man had to hurry to keep up with the lawman's lengthy strides. Once they were on the street in front of the station, Winchell whistled for a cab. Longarm had to give credit where credit was due. Being a city dweller, Winchell was pretty good at that job.

Half an hour later, they were sitting in the Metrolite's dining room with plates of steak, eggs, hash-browned potatoes, and flapjacks in front of them. Steam rose from the strong black brew in their coffee cups. Longarm had ordered for both of them, and Winchell looked dubiously at the mountain of food in front of him.

"I'm not sure I can eat all this," he said.

"Do you good," Longarm said. "A fella needs a hearty breakfast to keep him going."

"Yes, but there's enough food here for an army!"

Longarm pointed at Winchell's plate with his fork. "Just dig in."

Winchell did so, albeit reluctantly, and as they ate, Longarm went on, "Tell me about Angela Boothe."

Winchell swallowed. "I believe you're acquainted with her aunt and uncle, Lord and Lady Beechmuir?"

"So she's their niece, eh? All I knew was the name, figured she might be their daughter."

Winchell shook his head. "No, her father was Lord Beechmuir's younger brother. He lived for a time in the United States, since, of course, being the second son, he could not inherit the family estate."

"Remittance man, eh?" Longarm said with a nod. "I've run into a few of 'em. Most of 'em are pretty good hombres, but some of them turn bitter and get to be what them Britishers call rotters."

"Indeed. From what I know, Angela Boothe's father was the more solid sort. He eventually married an American woman and returned to England. Angela was their only child. Since both of her parents passed away a few years ago, Lord and Lady Beechmuir have been attempting to look after her. Unfortunately, she's a bit . . ." Winchell took a deep breath and then lowered his voice to a more discreet tone. "She's a bit wild, I'm afraid. There were instances in England that were, for want of a better word, shocking."

"Sounds like a good enough word to me," Longarm said. "What's she doing in the States? Did Lord and Lady Beechmuir send her over here to get her out of their hair?"

"Actually, when the trip was arranged through the State Department, it was described as a pleasure excursion so that Miss Boothe could see her mother's native country.

But in truth . . ." Winchell shrugged a shoulder. "What you say has a great deal of validity, Marshal."

Longarm drank some coffee. It was good, but it would have been even better with a slug of Maryland rye in it, he thought.

"So what's happened?" he asked. "Her uncle and aunt wanted her gone from England so that she wouldn't embarrass them. What's she done over here?"

"She's disappeared, that's what she's done. Dropped out of sight completely. The last time Lord and Lady Beechmuir heard from her was two weeks ago. Miss Boothe had been sending telegraph messages to them regularly before that. The last one came from here in Kansas City." Winchell glanced around. "In fact, she was staying here at the Metrolite Hotel."

"And they're worried about her?"

"Of course. Lord and Lady Beechmuir still love their niece, despite everything that happened in England. They want us to find her and make sure she's all right."

"If we find her, what happens then? Does she get sent back to England?"

"To be honest with you, Marshal, I have no idea," Winchell said. "In that case, we'll simply have to await further instructions. Or, I should say, I will await further instructions. If we succeed in locating Miss Boothe, your job is done and you can return to Denver."

Longarm nodded. He speared the last bite of flapjack with his fork and popped it into his mouth. So this was a simple missing persons case, he thought, and only the fact that Angela Boothe was related to British nobility made it important enough to bring the full weight of the State Department and the Justice Department to bear. If Angela had been an American girl, nobody would have cared all that much that she had vanished . . . unless, of course, her daddy was rich, or a powerful politician, or both.

Longarm shoved those thoughts out of his mind. Angela Boothe might be in danger, might even be dead. She was the one who was important here, not her uncle or aunt or anything else in her background.

"What else do you know about her?" he asked Winchell.

"Not much, unfortunately. I don't even have a photograph of her. There hasn't been enough time to get one from England. But I know she is twenty-three years of age, has blond hair, and is quite attractive in a, ah, buxom way."

Longarm grinned. "That's one of the best ways," he said as he reached for the last of his coffee.

"Yes, I suppose."

"You said she was staying here at this hotel. Did she check out before she vanished?"

Winchell shook his head. "No. When she hadn't been seen for several days, management checked her room, fearing the worst, even though no . . . unusual . . . odors had been reported. The room was empty. The bed had not been slept in, at least not recently."

"You checked at the train station?" Longarm asked.

"I did. No one answering Miss Boothe's description bought a ticket around the time she disappeared, at least not that any of the clerks recalled."

"That don't mean much," Longarm muttered. "Folks sometimes forget things, especially when they're busy."

"Yes, that's certainly true. And even if the clerks are remembering correctly, someone else could have bought a ticket for Miss Boothe. If she boarded without the assistance of a porter, it's possible no one at the depot would have noticed her."

"There are still a few stagecoach lines—" Longarm began.

"I checked them as well," Winchell said. "With the same results, or lack of results, I should say. It's almost as if Miss Boothe dropped off the face of the earth."

11

Longarm took out a cheroot and put it in his mouth. "What was her room number here?"

"Three twelve."

"I reckon the hotel has rented it out again since then?"

"There was no reason not to," Winchell said. "None of Miss Boothe's belongings were left behind in the room."

"So she either cleaned it out when she left . . . or somebody else cleaned it out after she was gone." A faintly grim edge crept into Longarm's voice as he spoke.

"Yes, the same thought occurred to me. I fear for Miss Boothe's safety, Marshal. I fear that she might already be deceased."

Longarm shoved his chair back. "Then we better get to looking. If it ain't too late already, sooner or later it will be."

# Chapter 3

Earlier, Longarm had dropped his valise in his room, which was on the second floor. Now, with Winchell trailing behind him, he walked up to the third floor, where Angela Boothe had stayed in room 312 while she was in Kansas City. The Metrolite was a nice place, not gaudy or overly fancy, but solidly built and comfortable. The third-floor corridor had a carpet runner in the middle of it and curtains over the window at the far end. Longarm walked to the window, flicked the curtains aside, and looked out. He saw that the Metrolite had one of the amenities that were starting to become common in hotels in larger cities, a set of fire escape stairs.

"This window been tampered with?" He didn't see any signs of forced entry around the window, but any damage could have been repaired by now.

"The manager of the hotel says no."

Longarm nodded and walked back down the hall to room 312. He bent and looked at the lock. Again, there were no signs that anyone had fooled with it, but a skilled cracksman could get past a lock like this without leaving much, if any, evidence behind.

"Same thing here, no damage to the lock or the jamb?"

Winchell shook his head. "None reported."

Longarm straightened. "Then either somebody's lying, or the room wasn't broken into."

"Are you saying that Miss Boothe must have left on her own, rather than being removed against her will?"

"Nope. Even if nobody busted in, she might've opened the door to a knock, had a gun shoved in her face, and been taken out that way." Longarm jerked a thumb toward the rear of the hotel. "I noticed some back stairs. If she was kidnapped in the middle of the night, likely nobody would have seen her being carried out."

Winchell took off his hat and ran his fingers through his fair hair. "Lord, I hate to think of that poor girl being abducted. I don't know her at all, of course, but I don't believe anyone should be subjected to such an ordeal."

Longarm liked Winchell a little better after the State Department man said that. Winchell was a stuffed shirt and a desk-riding bureaucrat, but he had some humanity in him, too.

The door of one of the other rooms along the corridor opened, and a hotel maid stepped out, carrying a stack of towels. She nodded as she came toward them and said, "Gentlemen, can I help you?"

"You work here on this floor regular-like?" Longarm asked her.

"Yes, of course." The maid was young and pretty, with long red hair pulled up in a bun under her starched cap.

Longarm inclined his head toward the door of room 312. "Do you remember a young woman who stayed in this room a couple of weeks ago? Blond, had an English accent, more than likely."

"Yes, the woman who disappeared. All the hotel staff is talking about it, even now."

Longarm glanced at Winchell. The fella might have some hidden talents, but carrying out a discreet investigation wasn't one of them.

14

"You don't have any idea what happened to her?"

The maid shook her head. "No, sir, I don't. Are you a policeman, sir? Surely you don't think I had anything to do with . . . with . . ."

Longarm held up a hand. "No need for you to worry, miss," he said. "You ain't in any trouble."

The maid heaved a sigh of relief. "Thank goodness. I was afraid that because I had bent the rules for her—"

"What do you mean by that?" Longarm cut in.

"Well, I'm supposed to tend to the rooms every day, of course. That's my job. But Miss Boothe asked me not to disturb her room, and I . . . well, I agreed." The maid lowered her voice. "I suspected she was entertaining a gentleman on a regular basis, and she didn't want anyone to see the evidence of her rendezvous."

"So she had a fella?" Longarm asked with a frown and a glance at Winchell. The State Department man lifted his shoulders in a shrug. Clearly, this was the first Winchell had heard of it.

"I don't know for sure, of course. It was just a feeling I had. I never saw anyone coming and going from her room other than Miss Boothe." The maid paused and then added, "Except, of course, for one time."

"Who did you see then?"

"That little French gentleman. At least, I think he was French. He had an accent."

Longarm looked at Winchell again, and this time the man from Washington just shook his head. Winchell was beginning to look upset, and Longarm didn't blame him. He'd found out more in an hour or so after arriving in Kansas City than Winchell had in several days of poking around.

Keeping his voice casual, Longarm asked, "This French fella, is he still staying here in the hotel?"

"No, he checked out a couple of days ago."

"What was his name?"

"I believe it was Mr. Dushane. I don't know his first name."

Longarm nodded. "I'm much obliged. You say he visited Miss Boothe here in her room?"

"Well, he was at the door one day. I don't know if he actually went inside or not."

"Were they friendly?"

"They weren't *un*friendly," the maid said. "But they didn't strike me as being that close, either. They were definitely acquainted, though. They weren't strangers."

"What happened after you saw them talking?"

"I don't know. I went in one of the other rooms to tend to my duties, and when I came out Mr. Dushane was gone and Miss Boothe's door was closed."

"Did you see Miss Boothe after that?"

A frown creased the redhead's brow. "Now that you mention it, sir, I don't believe I did. I think that was the last time I saw her."

"Good Lord," Winchell said breathlessly. "Marshal, do you think she was abducted by this French fellow, this Dushane?"

Before Longarm could answer, the maid said, "So you're a marshal. I knew you were some sort of policeman."

Longarm ignored that and said to Winchell, "Like the old hymn says, further along we'll know more about it. I reckon after we track down this Dushane and have ourselves a little talk with him."

"So we *are* working together," Winchell said with a smile.

"Looks like it," Longarm agreed. "For now, anyway."

According to the hotel register, Pierre Dushane, who gave his home address as Paris, France, had been in Kansas City on business, arriving three days after Angela Boothe and not departing until just three days earlier, which had

16

been more than a week after Angela's disappearance. The nature of his business was unspecified, and there was no indication of where he was going next.

Longarm could tell that the hotel manager was quite curious about his interest in Dushane, but the man curbed his curiosity. Longarm slid the register back across the counter and asked, "Did Dushane ever mention what line he was in?"

"No, sir," the manager replied. "He was quiet, stayed in his room a lot, didn't talk to the hotel staff any more than he had to. I thought he was an exemplary guest. I wish all the people who stop over with us were so easy to accommodate."

"He didn't leave any forwarding address for mail?"

"No. He didn't receive any mail while he was here, or telegrams or any other sort of communication, as far as I remember. Obviously, he wasn't expecting any to come after he left, or he would have given us a forwarding address."

"What did he look like?"

The description of Dushane that the manager gave Longarm and Winchell matched what the redheaded maid had told them. Dushane was short, slender, in his forties, and very respectable-looking. He was a natty dresser and had graying sandy hair and a neatly trimmed mustache. Longarm couldn't see any obvious connection between a middle-aged Frenchman and an attractive young Englishwoman who was apparently something of a hellion, but unless the maid had been wrong about what she had seen, there had to be one.

Longarm thanked the hotel manager, then he and Winchell left the Metrolite. "What do we do now?" Winchell asked.

"We cover the same ground you did when you were asking about Miss Boothe," Longarm told him. "Only this

17

time we try to find out if Dushane left Kansas City on a train or stagecoach."

"He was at the hotel for more than a week after Miss Boothe disappeared," Winchell pointed out. "If he did abduct her, do you think he was holding her prisoner for all that time?"

"Could be," Longarm said grimly. "If she wasn't already dead and buried somewhere. . . ."

# Chapter 4

Pierre Dushane proved to be as elusive as Angela Boothe. Longarm and Winchell spent the day checking out every possibility they could think of. As far as they could tell, Dushane had not left Kansas City by train or stagecoach, nor had he rented a horse from any of the livery stables. Either he had departed some other way, or he was still in the city.

"What's our next move, Marshal Long?" Winchell asked over supper that evening in the hotel dining room.

"There's a heap of other hotels and boardinghouses in Kansas City," Longarm said. "Did you check them to see if Miss Boothe was staying at any of them?"

Winchell looked a little crestfallen. "You know, I didn't. I never thought of it. I was convinced she had left town, or been taken away, but there's no evidence of that. So you're saying we should make the rounds of everywhere else she could be staying?"

"Her and Dushane both." Longarm nodded. "By the way, my front handle is Custis, and some folks call me Longarm. I reckon if we're gonna be pards, you ought to start calling me one or the other."

Winchell's face lit up as he said, "Pards? Really? That

19

would be splendid, Marshal . . . I mean, Longarm . . . Longarm," he repeated. "I rather like that. It suits you."

The big lawman grinned. "Well, as my old ma back in West-by-God Virginia used to say, you can call me anything you want, just don't call me late for supper."

"I don't understand," Winchell said with a frown. "We're eating supper now, aren't we?"

"It's just an old saying, Stewart." Longarm took out a cheroot and reached for another. "Smoke?"

"Oh, no, thank you. I never use tobacco."

"How about we find a saloon and have a drink, then?" Longarm stuck the cheroot in his mouth and asked around it, "You do drink, don't you?"

"Certainly. I enjoy a glass of port or Madeira every now and then."

"Ever had any Tom Moore?"

"I don't think so. What sort of liquor is that?"

"Maryland rye," Longarm said, practically smacking his lips over the words. "Smooth as silk, but it'll start a blaze in your innards."

"Well"—Winchell looked a little dubious—"I must give it a try."

They walked down the street to a saloon, and when they came back out an hour later, Winchell was a bit wobbly on his feet. Longarm had to take the government man's arm to steady him.

"My, you were right, Marshal," Winchell said. "I mean Longarm. That Maryland rye has caused a v-veritable inferno in my innards." He laughed. "An inferno in my innards. What a delightful turn of phrase, if I do say so myself."

"Come on, old son," Longarm said with a grin. "You got a mite carried away. You need a good night's sleep, because you're going to feel pretty peaked in the morning."

Longarm guided Winchell through the lobby of the

Metrolite and up the stairs to the second floor. Winchell's room was directly across the hall from Longarm's. With considerable difficulty, Winchell finally fitted the key in the lock and turned it. Out of habit, Longarm tensed a little as the door swung open. His right hand moved a bit closer to the butt of the Colt .45 in a crossdraw rig on his left hip. You never knew what might come out of a darkened hotel room. Sometimes it was a knife or a bullet.

Tonight it was neither. Winchell's room was empty. Longarm lit the lamp on a side table as Winchell stumbled over to the bed and threw himself facedown on it, fully dressed. He was snoring by the time Longarm straightened from the lamp.

Longarm shook his head as he looked at the sleeping State Department man. He supposed he should have kept Winchell from drinking so much, but hell, the fella was a grown man, Longarm told himself.

And he was going to have a man-sized headache come morning, too.

Longarm left Winchell's room and stepped into the corridor, intending to cross to his own room. Before he could do so, however, a woman's voice hailed him from down the hall, saying, "Marshal, wait a minute."

He turned and saw a young woman with long red hair coming toward him. She wore a gray woolen dress that clung to her slender but amply curved figure, and it took him a second to recognize her with her hair down and without the maid's uniform.

"Howdy," he said. "You work on this floor, too?"

"Yes, but I'm not working now," the young woman said. "I was looking for you."

"You remembered something else about that gal my partner and me are looking for?"

She moved closer to him and laid a hand on her arm. The fingers bore the marks of the work she did, but they were still slender and supple. "No, I'm afraid I've told you all I know about that. I just wanted to see you again."

Longarm smiled. "Some folks would say that was a mite forward of you, ma'am."

Her hand moved up his arm and then reached to the back of his neck as she moved even closer to him, so close that he felt the warmth of her body through their clothes. "I work in a hotel, Marshal," she said. "I know what goes on here. Some of the people who would look down their noses at me and call me a trollop because I tell you that I find you attractive are the same people who do things here that would shame a billy goat. I just believe in being honest about what I feel . . . and what I want."

"Then I'd say that you and me are pretty much in agreement, ma'am," Longarm said, and then he brought his mouth down on hers in a passionate kiss.

"Grace," she said when their lips parted a long moment later. "My name is Grace."

"And it suits you mighty fine," Longarm told her. He had his key in his hand, and a moment later they were inside the room with the door swinging shut behind them.

He lit the lamp, turned it low so that only a soft yellow glow filled the room. Then Grace moved into his arms and he kissed her again, tasting the hot, wet sweetness of her mouth with his tongue as her lips parted. Her full breasts pressed warmly against his chest. His manhood swelled inside his trousers, quickly growing into a spike that thrust against the buttons of his fly. Grace reached down and began to unfasten those buttons. When his shaft was freed from the tight confines of his trousers, it jutted out proudly from his groin and prodded her soft belly. She caressed the long, thick pole and moaned with longing.

"My God," she whispered as she leaned against him. "I have to have that thing inside me."

"I'll be mighty happy to oblige, ma'am," Longarm said as he cupped her left breast through her dress and ran his thumb over the hard bud of her erect nipple. "I reckon we'd better get out of these clothes first, though."

"That's the best idea I've heard all night, Marshal."

He was going to tell her to call him Custis or Longarm, but that seemed like too much of a waste of time and energy they could use for other, more pleasurable things. They got to work, peeling each other's clothes off in short order until both of them were nude. Then Longarm drew her into his embrace again, holding her and kissing her as he reached down to cup the soft swells of her buttocks. She ground her pelvis against his organ where it was trapped between them. The thatch of dark red hair that covered her triangle teased the sensitive flesh of his manhood.

Longarm moved them to the bed and eased Grace down on it. He bent over her and sucked one of her nipples into his mouth, running his tongue around it and then biting it lightly. She ran her fingers through his hair as he did so. He moved to the other breast and licked and sucked that nipple as well. His hand slid over her belly and moved between her legs. Her thighs opened wider. He stroked the damp folds of flesh at the center of her femininity and slipped a finger into her as he thumbed the tiny bud at the top of her opening. Her hips bucked up off the mattress, and she cried out softly as he continued to caress her.

She wrapped both hands around his shaft and tugged him into position between her wide-flung thighs. Longarm rubbed the head up and down her dew-covered crease and then slowly insinuated it, penetrating her bit by bit until he had several inches inside her.

"All of it," she panted. "I want all of it!"

He gave it to her with a driving surge of his hips that sheathed most of his organ inside her. She cried out again and thrust up at him. He drove into her again, delving even deeper, plumbing depths that, to judge by her reaction, had never been plumbed before. She locked her arms and legs around him and pulled him even closer. Their lips met, and then their tongues dueled fiercely and sensuously as he launched into a timeless rhythm, in and out.

Within moments the tide of desire in them began to crest. Longarm felt his climax boiling up and did nothing to slow it, sensing that Grace wouldn't want him to delay. She was every bit as worked up and in need of release as he was. He surged into her for a final time and then held his shaft there, as deeply inside her as he could go. His culmination burst from him, filling her with spurt after white-hot spurt of his seed. Her juices gushed as well, soaking both of them.

Longarm held her tightly as they slid down the far side of the slope together. He was completely drained, and Grace was, too. He rolled onto his side, still holding her, and after a few minutes both of them drifted off to sleep.

# Chapter 5

"Oh, my dear sweet Lord," Stewart Winchell said in a voice that was half groan. He propped his elbows on the table and gently lowered his head into the palms of his hands, holding it there as if afraid that it was about to topple right off his shoulders if he didn't hang on tight. "Why didn't you stop me from drinking so much, Longarm?"

From where he was seated across the table in the hotel dining room, Longarm said, "I'm sorry, Stewart. I reckon I should have warned you that you were putting away too much of that Tom Moore." He tried not to grin. He knew how Winchell felt. When he was just a youngster, he had gone on a bender a time or two and had woken up the next morning with one hell of a hangover. It had been a long time, though, since liquor had had that much of an effect on him. He supposed he had built up a tolerance for the stuff.

"You certainly should have warned me," Winchell scolded him without looking up. "But to be fair, I'm not sure I would have believed you. I think I was too far gone after that first drink."

"Well, there's a pot of black coffee on the way. Drink

plenty of it, and eat something if you can."

Winchell groaned again. "I'm not sure I can eat. Just the thought of it makes me queasy."

"You'll be all right," Longarm assured him. "It just takes a little time."

Time was something they might not have, he reminded himself. As long as Angela Boothe was missing, there was a chance the young woman was in danger. Time could be running out for her. . . .

Longarm had awoken early that morning with Grace's warm, lithe body still snuggled next to him, spoon fashion. He had cupped her breasts and slipped his shaft into her from behind for a bout of slow, sweet lovemaking, and she told him later, as she kissed him just before leaving his room, that it had been the best way of waking up she had ever known. Longarm couldn't argue with that.

He was already in the dining room when Winchell came in, moving like a hundred-year-old man whose bones were about to snap in two. The State Department man's face was as gray as a mud dauber's nest, and about the same consistency, too.

After a few minutes a white-aproned waitress brought the pot of coffee and the breakfast Longarm had already ordered. Longarm had the woman fetch another cup for Winchell, who insisted that he couldn't eat anything, not even a bite. Longarm didn't argue with him but lit into the food instead. He was as hungry as a bear.

Winchell sipped coffee, grimaced, and then choked down a little more of the hot black brew. After a few minutes, he said, "I might be able to eat a little piece of one of those flapjacks. Only a bite, mind you."

Longarm tore off half a flapjack and handed it to him. "Here you go."

Winchell nibbled on it, drank some more coffee, and ate some more. His face was still gray, but not as much so. A little color was creeping back into it. "What are our plans for today?" he asked.

"Check the hotels and boardinghouses for Miss Boothe and that Dushane fella. I reckon we'll have to split up to do it, otherwise it'll take too long."

Winchell nodded. "All right. I feel a bit better now. You can count on me, Longarm."

"I know I can. You'll do just fine."

Winchell looked bleary-eyed at him. "There's just one thing I want you to promise me."

"What's that?"

"If you ever see me about to take more than one drink again, take out that gun of yours and shoot me, then and there. I'd rather be put out of my misery than suffer these infernal imps cavorting inside my skull."

"Deal," Longarm said with a grin.

Winchell borrowed a city directory from the owner of the Metrolite and made a list of the other hotels and boardinghouses in Kansas City. Longarm knew the town well enough from previous visits so that he was able to help Winchell split up the list geographically. Longarm took the places on the west side of Kansas City, Winchell those on the east side. They would meet back at the Metrolite that evening.

As he hoofed it up and down the streets, Longarm found himself thinking he was damned glad he wasn't a city policeman. He would hate spending all his time in a place like this. He'd been here only a couple of days, and already he found himself missing the wide-open spaces, the plains and the mountains and the deserts of the West that were his home, even though he hadn't been born out there. To put it simply, he was a frontiersman, and Kansas City was just too damned *civilized*.

His frustration also grew as the day passed, because everywhere he asked about Angela Boothe and Pierre Dushane and described them, he got blank looks and shakes of the head. No one had seen them; no one knew anything about them. It was as Winchell had said—they seemed to have vanished off the face of the earth.

The sun had set and early evening had draped itself over the city when Longarm returned to the Metrolite. He found Winchell sitting at a table in the lobby, looking at a piece of paper. Winchell seemed tired and dispirited, but he appeared to have recovered from his hangover. Longarm recognized the document as Winchell's half of the list of places to search. As he came closer, he saw that the government man had drawn lines through every hotel and boardinghouse on the list.

"No luck, eh?" Longarm asked as he walked up to the table.

Winchell shook his head. "I hope you have more to report than I do."

"Nope, afraid not."

"Then we've failed. Utterly and completely."

"Don't get too down in the mouth about it," Longarm said. "We'll keep looking."

"Where?"

"Well, we'll talk about that over supper."

Winchell pushed himself to his feet. "I'd like to go up and change my shirt. I've been tramping around all day, and it got rather warm."

"Sure," Longarm agreed. "I'll go up to my room and wash up a mite myself."

Together, the two men climbed the stairs and started down the empty second-floor corridor toward their rooms. When they reached them, Winchell unlocked his door first. Longarm paused for a second, looking down to see if the matchstick he had wedged between the door and the jamb when he left that morning was still in place. It was, signifying that no one had snuck into his room while he was gone.

He was about to slide his key into the lock when he heard a weak, strained voice call, "Custis . . ." He turned his head toward the voice, and his eyes widened with shock as he saw Grace stumble out of an alcove at the end of the hall. She had her hands pressed to her midsection, where her maid's uniform had a large, ugly red stain on it.

Longarm took a step toward her, saying, "Grace, what the hell—"

At that moment, behind him, Stewart Winchell stepped into his darkened room, and Colt flame bloomed in the shadows as several shots hammered out. Longarm heard the roar and pivoted, his hand instinctively flashing across his body to palm the Colt from its holster as he did so. He turned in time to see Winchell flung back out into the corridor by the bullets smashing into him.

Winchell backpedaled fast across the hall and hit the door of Longarm's room. He hung there for a second or two, looking down at his chest. The white breast of his shirt was now crimson from the blood that welled out of the bullet wounds. Winchell let out a soft sigh and began to slide down the door. Longarm saw the life go out of his eyes. He was dead by the time he hit the floor.

Biting back a curse, Longarm flung himself into a rolling dive that took him past the open door of Winchell's room. The Colt bucked in his hand as he triggered three shots as fast as he could.

More gun-flame stabbed from inside the room as Winchell's killer—or killers—returned Longarm's fire. Longarm came out of the roll and surged onto his feet. He pressed his back against the wall and watched the door. From the corner of his eye he could see Winchell's body, and he also saw that Grace had slumped to the carpet runner at the far end of the hall. He couldn't help Winchell now, but he wanted to go to Grace and see what he could do for her. If he did, though, he would be exposing himself to more shots from inside the room.

Suddenly, he heard a window thrust up, followed by the sounds of someone clambering through it. The bastards were getting away. He went to the floor again in a sliding dive that carried him into the open doorway. The room was still dark inside, but he could see the window—and the silhouette of the man who was batting aside the curtains and trying to climb through it.

"Hold it!" Longarm snapped.

The man, halfway out the window, twisted and brought his gun up. Orange fire lanced from the muzzle. The slug ripped a gash in the carpet runner and kicked up splinters from the floorboards not far from Longarm's head. Coolly, the big lawman fired twice. With a grunt of pain, the figure in the window doubled over and then toppled backward. The bushwhacker's head struck the bottom of the pane that had been shoved up, and glass shattered under the impact. The man fell the rest of the way through the window.

As the echoes of the shots faded, Longarm heard running footsteps in the alley outside. There had been more than one of them, and the other men had gotten away.

He could check on the man he had shot and go after the others later. Right now, he was worried about Grace. He sprang to his feet and ran down the hall toward her bloody, fallen form.

# Chapter 6

Grace's green eyes flickered open as Longarm dropped to a knee beside her and lifted her head. He slid his arm under her shoulders to support her as he raised her into a half-sitting position. Her face was pale, making the tiny freckles on it stand out. She looked up at Longarm and gasped, "Custis! You . . . you're all right?"

"I'm fine, but we got to see about getting a doctor for you," he said. "What happened? How bad are you hurt?"

He thought he already knew the answer to that last question. Grace's dress was sodden with blood . . . too much blood for her to survive losing it.

"Th-three men . . . they came up the back stairs . . . jumped me. . . . One of them had . . . a Bowie knife . . . he cut me . . . hurt me . . . said he'd kill me if I didn't tell him . . . which room you were in."

The already bleak cast of Longarm's features intensified even more. The carnage that had taken place in this hallway was because of him. He was the one the killers had been after.

"I . . . I didn't tell them," Grace went on. "Said you were in . . . the room . . . across the hall."

She had protected him, he thought, but in doing so, she

31

had doomed Stewart Winchell. The bushwhackers had started shooting as soon as Winchell opened the door, thinking they were ambushing Longarm.

"I'm sorry . . . about your friend . . . but I couldn't . . . couldn't let them hurt you."

"Just take it easy now," Longarm muttered. "I reckon somebody probably went for the doctor already."

"Too late. . . . After I told them . . . the man with the knife . . . stuck it all the way in me . . . ripped me apart inside . . . I can feel it, Custis . . . I'm dying. . . ."

"Hush now," Longarm said. "You're going to be just fine."

But he knew she was right. He saw the life ebbing away from her as she whispered, "Never knew anybody . . . like you before. . . . So glad I . . ."

Then she was gone, her eyes glazing over as she stared up at the ceiling of the corridor without seeing it.

Gently, he lowered her to the carpet. A huge anger filled him. The bushwhackers had murdered this innocent girl, and they had blasted the life out of Stewart Winchell, whom Longarm had come to consider a friend despite his eastern ways. Standing, Longarm swung back toward the stairs that led down to the lobby.

Several men stood there, including the desk clerk and the owner of the Metrolite. They stared in horror at the bodies of Winchell and Grace. Longarm broke into their shocked stupor by saying sharply, "Has somebody gone for a doctor?"

The hotel owner jerked and said, "Y-yes. I sent a boy right away as soon as I heard the shots. Are . . . are they . . ."

"They're dead," Longarm said heavily. "The sawbones will be too late. What about the law?"

"The police should be here shortly, too."

Longarm nodded. "When they get here, tell them I've gone out back to the alley. I'm pretty sure I ventilated one of the skunks as he was trying to get out through the window, and that ought to be where he landed."

"Marshal Long!" the owner called after him, but Longarm ignored the man as he stalked over to the rear stairs and clattered down them.

His Colt was reloaded and in his hand again as he stepped out the rear door into the shadowy alley. He had emptied the spent shells from the cylinder and thumbed in fresh cartridges as he went down the stairs. He was careful as he advanced along the alley toward the spot that would be underneath the window in Winchell's room, but nobody shot at him. That didn't really surprise him. The gunmen had probably figured out that their ambush had gone all wrong, and he figured the two survivors had taken off for the tall and uncut.

Spotting a dark shape lying huddled on the ground, he stopped and trained the Colt on it. The twisted figure wasn't moving, though. After a moment Longarm fished a lucifer out of his vest pocket and ignited it with a snap of his thumbnail. Squinting his eyes against the glare, he studied the body of the man he had shot.

From the looks of it, he had gotten the gent once in the chest and once in the belly. He wished that chest wound had been a little lower. It had probably killed the bushwhacker pretty quickly, so that he didn't have to endure the agony of being gut-shot like he deserved. Besides, if the man had still been alive, he might have been able to answer some questions before he died.

He was dead, though, no doubt about that. His eyes were wide and glassy. He was dressed in rough, workingman's clothes, and a battered derby lay on the ground beside him. His features were craggy and unshaven. A typical city tough, ready, willing, and able to do just about anything—including torturing a girl and ambushing a lawman—if the money was right.

"You there!" a voice called. "Don't move!"

Longarm glanced over his shoulder and saw several blue-uniformed Kansas City policemen hurrying toward him, guns drawn. Just before the lucifer burned down and he had to drop it, he said, "Take it easy, boys. We're on the same side. I'm a deputy United States marshal, name of Custis Long."

"That's what Mr. Parmenter said," one of the policemen replied, "but we're going to need to see some identification."

Longarm knew that Parmenter was the owner of the hotel. He said, "One of you strike a fresh match, then, and I'll be glad to show you my bona fides."

Establishing his identity took only a few moments. Once the trio of policemen were satisfied that he was indeed a federal lawman, one of them studied the dead man's face in the light of a match and exclaimed, "That's Ted Sparling!"

"You know him, do you?" Longarm said.

"Yes, he's a rough character. Been suspected of several violent crimes in the past, but he's never been convicted of anything. Not here in Kansas City, anyway."

"Him and two other fellas hid in a hotel room they thought was mine," Longarm explained. "It really belonged to a friend of mine, and when he went in, they opened fire on him and killed him."

"That would be Mr. Winchell?"

Longarm nodded. "That's right. He never had a chance. They bushwhacked him without any warning. And before that they tortured and killed a girl who worked in the hotel as a maid."

"Grace Dugan," the local officer who seemed to be the spokesman said. "We saw her body as well. I sent a man for the undertaker. He's going to be quite busy tonight."

"I reckon. Does this fella"—Longarm gestured at the dead Sparling—"run with anybody in particular?"

"You're thinking about the other two men who were with him tonight?"

"Them are the ones I had in mind," Longarm replied grimly.

"We know his usual associates, but it's our job to find them, Marshal, not yours."

"It was me they were trying to kill," Longarm pointed out. He wasn't going to like it if this Kansas City copper tried to shut him out of the investigation.

"Murder is a local matter, not federal."

"But it's a federal case they interfered with," Longarm said. "How about we go look for 'em together?"

The policeman considered that for a moment, then shrugged and nodded. "I suppose you have a right to accompany us. Like you said, you were the intended victim. And you're a lawman, too, so as a professional courtesy . . ."

"I'm much obliged. Now, who are these skunks, and where do we find 'em?"

"Sparling could usually be found with Bill Horne and Luther Jackson. They have rooms above a tavern called Red Mike's." The policeman detailed one of his companions to stay with Sparling's body, then led Longarm and the other copper out of the alley. "By the way, I'm Constable Ed Gibson. This is Constable Tom Tinsley."

Longarm nodded curtly. "Under other circumstances, I'd say I was glad to meet you fellas. As it is, though . . ."

"I understand, Marshal," Gibson said. "Murder never makes for pleasant acquaintances."

Longarm stuck an unlit cheroot in his mouth as he walked along the street with the two officers. "What can you tell me about Sparling and the other two?" he asked.

"I already said that Sparling has a bad reputation. He's actually the best of the three. He works sometimes at the railroad station, but Horne and Jackson have no obvious means of support. Yet they always have money."

"Which means they're crooks, more than likely."

Gibson nodded. "That's what those of us on the force believe, anyway. They're violent, ill-tempered men who are known to have killed other men, but they've always gotten away with pleading self-defense."

"One of them in the habit of carrying a Bowie knife?"

"That would be Luther Jackson."

"He's the one who killed Miss Dugan," Longarm said, his voice tight with suppressed rage. "I got that right from her own lips before she died."

"That's good enough evidence for me," Gibson said. "We'll arrest Jackson for murder and bring Horne in for questioning."

That was assuming the two men would let themselves be arrested without a fight, Longarm thought. He had a feeling that was pretty unlikely, but he was willing to let things play out however they might. He was a lawman, not a vigilante, and he couldn't go in shooting. Like it or not, he had to give the bastards a chance to surrender.

Besides, he needed at least one of them alive to answer some questions. He was in Kansas City for only one reason: to find Angela Boothe. He didn't know any of the three men who had tried to bushwhack him, so that meant they could have had only one reason for wanting him dead.

To keep him from finding Angela Boothe . . .

"There it is," Constable Gibson said a few minutes later as they turned a corner. "Red Mike's."

# Chapter 7

During his years as a lawman, Longarm had seen hundreds of dives like this one, squalid places where men dulled the pain of their existence by guzzling down cheap, rotgut liquor. There were usually a few disease-ridden whores available, too, for even more transitory pleasures. The air was thick with tobacco smoke, but that wasn't enough to completely cover up the eternal stench of urine, vomit, and stale beer. It was noisy inside, with lots of loud talk and raucous laughter, but the place went dead quiet as soon as the patrons realized that the law had come in.

Longarm wouldn't know Horne and Jackson if he saw them, but he assumed that the two policemen with him would. He looked around the main room with its sawdust-covered floor, rough tables and chairs, and a scarred wooden bar along the left-hand wall. Oil lamps hung from the ceiling and gave off a hazy glow. To the right, a dark, narrow staircase led up to the second floor, and Longarm remembered Gibson's comment about the two men they were seeking having rooms up there.

"I don't see them, Ed," Constable Tinsley said.

"Neither do I," Gibson replied. He walked over to a

burly man in a dirty apron who stood behind the bar. The bartender had a drooping mustache and a tangled mass of dark hair. "Glover, I'm looking for Bill Horne and Luther Jackson. Have you seen them tonight?"

"Those boys come an' go as they please, Constable," Glover replied. "You know that. I ain't paid no attention, and I ain't seen 'em."

"You could hardly miss them if they came in and went upstairs." Gibson's voice was mild, but it had a core of steel in it. His hand wasn't far from the gun on his hip.

"I tell you, I ain't seen 'em," the bartender insisted.

"Then it's all right if we go upstairs and have a look around?"

Glover shrugged his broad shoulders. "Sure, it don't matter none to me. I can guarantee that some of the fellas up there with their gals won't be very happy about bein' disturbed, though."

"I'll take my chances," Gibson said dryly.

"Everybody does when they come to Red Mike's."

The two policemen and Longarm turned away from the bar and started making their way across the room toward the stairs. Longarm had been watching, and none of the men in the tavern had tried to slip up those stairs to carry a warning to Horne and Jackson, if indeed the two bushwhackers were really up there.

Longarm's gut told him they were, and over the years he had learned to trust his instincts.

All three lawmen drew their guns as they started up the narrow staircase. The upper hall at the top of the stairs was dimly lit, probably by a single candle stuck on a shelf somewhere. Longarm glanced back over his shoulder. This would be a hell of a place for an ambush, he thought. There would be no place for him and the two city star packers to go if anybody opened fire on them.

No sooner had the thought gone through Longarm's mind than a dark shape loomed against the faint light at

38

the top of the stairs. "Look out!" snapped Gibson, who was in the lead.

Longarm saw the rifle in the hands of the man above them but couldn't get a shot at him. Gibson was the only one with a chance. The policeman's gun roared just as the rifle blasted. Even over the deafening echoes of the shots, Longarm heard the soggy thud of a bullet striking flesh. Gibson grunted and went to his knees.

That gave Longarm, who was right behind him, the chance to fire. The Colt bucked twice in his hand as he triggered the shots. But the rifleman had already ducked back, and Longarm's slugs angled up and struck high on the wall on the far side of the landing.

"Ed!" Tinsley yelled at his fellow officer. "Ed, are you hit!"

Longarm vaulted over Gibson's slumped form and barked an order over his shoulder at Tinsley. "Look after him!" Then he was lunging up the stairs.

He knew he might be running right into the rifleman's sights, but he was too mad to hold back. The men upstairs had killed Winchell and Grace, and they might know something about the disappearance of Angela Boothe. Longarm couldn't let them get away.

Just before he reached the top of the stairs, he launched himself into a dive that carried him onto the landing. Twisting to the left, he brought up his revolver and looked for a target. The corridor was empty.

But not for long. A man rushed at him from the other direction. The slap of shoe leather on the bare planks of the hallway floor was his only warning. He rolled over again and saw a man leaping toward him, Bowie knife upraised in his hand for a killing stroke. The heavy blade flashed down, barely missing Longarm. With a shivering impact, the point of the knife hit the floor and embedded itself in the wood.

Longarm swung the Colt in a backhand blow that

caught the knife wielder on the jaw. The man was slammed back into the wall, blood streaming from the gash that the gunsight had opened up. He started to fall but caught his balance with a hand splayed against the faded and peeling wallpaper. His other hand clawed for the gun on his hip.

Longarm fired from the floor, sending a slug tearing through the man's shoulder. The man screamed and bounced off the wall to fall to his knees. Longarm kicked him in the chest and sent him sprawling on his back.

The rifle blasted again. A bullet whined past Longarm's head. He threw himself to the side, toward the stairs, and wound up tumbling down several of them before he was able to stop his fall. He scrambled back up and risked a look around the corner.

The man with the rifle must have ducked into one of the rooms earlier. Now he was on his way toward a window at the far end of the corridor, obviously intending to make his escape by such a route for the second time tonight. Assuming that the man with the Bowie knife was Luther Jackson, as Constable Gibson had said, that meant the fleeing man was Bill Horne.

"Horne!" Longarm shouted. "Stop or I'll fire!" He aimed at Horne's leg, intending to bring him down by wounding him.

Before Horne could reach the window, the pane was thrust up suddenly and a man stuck his head and shoulders through the opening. Horne skidded to a stop and brought up the rifle, loosing a wild shot toward the window. Shards of glass sprayed through the air as the bullet shattered the upper pane. The man at the window fired a pistol just as Horne darted to the side. Horne's head jerked violently. He dropped the rifle and spun around. Blood sprayed in a crimson circle from the bullet-torn artery in his neck and splattered the walls. Horne clawed at the hideous wound and lurched back and forth, ramming senselessly into one wall and then the other before falling to the floor, where he twitched out his misbegotten life in a matter of seconds.

Longarm leveled his Colt at the window, but the stranger who had shot Horne was gone. A place like Red Mike's was so far down the scale from the Metrolite that it wouldn't have a fire escape, so the stranger must have climbed a ladder to the upper floor.

Longarm checked on Jackson, who seemed to be unconscious. He twisted his head and looked down the stairs. Tinsley had pulled the wounded Gibson into a sitting position and was crouched beside him, gun in hand, covering the bottom of the stairs so that none of the men in the tavern below could get involved in the fracas. Gibson's eyes were open. He seemed conscious and coherent.

He proved that a second later by asking, "Marshal Long, are you all right?"

"I'm not hit," Longarm said. "Looks like Horne is dead, though, and Jackson's wounded." He pushed himself to his feet and stepped toward Jackson, covering the man as he approached.

Jackson's face was pale and twisted in pain. His jaw was swollen and covered with blood where Longarm had hit him with the Colt. The jaw might even be broken, which would make talking more difficult for him.

But he *would* talk, Longarm thought. Damn straight he would.

Longarm grasped Jackson's wounded shoulder and shook it. The man cried out in agony, roused from his stupor by the pain. Longarm's face might have been carved from stone. Jackson was the man who had tortured and murdered Grace Dugan, and the fact that Longarm needed him to talk was the only thing keeping him alive.

Well, that and a devotion to the law, Longarm mused . . . and under the circumstances, that devotion might have been stretched a whole heap.

"Jackson!" Longarm said sharply, trying to get through to the man. "Jackson, wake up!"

Jackson tried to focus bleary, pain-filled eyes on the man who knelt beside him.

"Listen to me, Jackson," Longarm went on. "Who paid you to bushwhack me? Where's Angela Boothe?"

Jackson opened his mouth, but all that came out was a thin cry of pain as shattered bone grated together in his jaw. Longarm grabbed his chin, which made Jackson whimper even harder, and jammed the barrel of the Colt into the soft hollow of his throat.

"I'm gonna let go of you in a minute," Longarm said, "and then you're gonna tell me what I want to know. If you don't, I'll make you hurt so much you'll beg me to pull the trigger and send a bullet up through your brain. You got that, Jackson?"

The wounded man couldn't nod, but Longarm saw the assent in his eyes.

Longarm let go of Jackson's jaw but kept the gun on him. Jackson struggled to form coherent words. "Stock . . ." he managed. "Stock . . . man . . ."

"You mean a rancher?" Longarm asked.

"Try . . . dent . . . try . . ."

"Try to dent what? Damn it, make sense!"

"Gone," Jackson mumbled. "Gone . . . to the devil . . ."

Suddenly, his back arched, his eyes opened wide, and a soundless scream came out of his mouth. He slumped down, a final breath rattling in his throat, and Longarm knew he was dead.

But that wasn't right. Jackson hadn't lost enough blood from either the wound in his shoulder or the gash on his jaw so that he should have died from it. Longarm checked for a pulse but found none. It didn't make any sense.

Until Longarm rolled him onto his side and found the Bowie knife, driven into Jackson's body at an angle. When Longarm had kicked him and knocked him backward, Jackson must have fallen on the knife that was still stuck in the floor of the corridor. It had come loose, twisted around somehow, and sliced into the body of its owner, finally penetrating to a vital spot as Longarm tried to question Jackson. Longarm let go of Jackson's shoulder and allowed the man to fall on his back again. Grim-faced with disappointment, Longarm came to his feet.

He had wanted more from Jackson, he thought, but at least he had something now. It might not add up to much, but it was better than nothing.

He had something besides Jackson's dying words to think about, too. During the brief but intense flurry of violence in the hallway, Longarm had gotten only a fleeting look at the man in the window who had killed Bill Horne. The man had been a stranger to Longarm, and the light had been bad, but Longarm was pretty sure he'd had graying sandy hair and a mustache. How the man had come to be at Red Mike's at just the right time to take a shot at Horne was still unknown, but Longarm felt reasonably certain he had just caught himself a glimpse of the mysterious Pierre Dushane.

# Chapter 8

Horne's rifle shot from the top of the stairs had knocked a chunk of meat out of Constable Gibson's side, but Tinsley had used a wadded-up handkerchief to slow the bleeding and ordered one of the men in the tavern to go fetch an ambulance wagon. Tinsley and Longarm helped Gibson to one of the tables and got him into a chair.

"It's a shame you were forced to kill both of them," Gibson said to Longarm. "At least you were able to question Jackson before he died."

"Yeah, but he didn't give me much to go on." Longarm didn't correct Gibson's assumption that he had gunned down both of the killers. He was the only one who had seen the man he took to be Dushane, so he was going to keep the knowledge of the Frenchman's involvement to himself for the time being. "He said something about a rancher and told me to try to dent something. I don't know what the hell he meant by that. Then he said he'd gone to the devil. At least, I reckon that's what he was trying to say."

"We already knew that he'd gone to the devil," Gibson said. "He was a terrible man and deserves to burn in Hell for what he's done."

Remembering what had happened to Grace Dugan, Longarm couldn't argue with that.

A short time later, the ambulance wagon rattled to a stop outside Red Mike's . . . probably not the first time it had come there on such an errand. Gibson was loaded in the back by the attendants and driven off to the hospital.

The undertaker's wagon showed up just as the ambulance was rolling out of sight.

Longarm watched as the bodies of Horne and Jackson were carried out of the tavern and loaded into the wagon. He lit a cheroot and drew the smoke into his lungs, frowning as he thought about everything that had happened. The way Luther Jackson had been mumbling because of that busted jaw, it had been hard to understand him, and Longarm found himself wondering if he had heard the man correctly. What else could Jackson have said, though?

Longarm was still convinced there was some connection between Angela Boothe's disappearance and the attempt on his life. That was the only thing that made any sense. Gibson had said that Ted Sparling, the man who had been killed at the Metrolite, had worked on occasion at the railroad station. Was it possible that Angela could have been smuggled out of Kansas City by train, and that the person or persons behind it had paid off Sparling and the other two toughs to kill anybody who came looking for her?

Longarm wasn't completely convinced that he had stumbled onto the answer, but the theory made sense. He would have to look harder at the train station. He had a couple of other ideas tickling around in the back of his brain, too. The Western Union office would be closed at this time of night, but as soon as it opened in the morning, he was going to send a wire to Billy Vail in Denver and see if Vail could find out the answers to a couple of questions.

"You want a drink?" the burly bartender called Glover

asked as Longarm watched the last of the undertaker's helpers leaving the tavern.

Longarm looked at the man and shook his head. "No, thanks. I would like to know if you warned Horne and Jackson somehow, though."

Glover held up his hands, palms out. "Hell, no, Marshal!" he replied vehemently. "I reckon maybe I stretched the truth a little . . . I did see those two come into the tavern and then go upstairs. But you know how it is in a place like this. A fella don't tell the law any more than he has to. I swear I didn't do anything to warn them, though."

Longarm reined in a surge of anger. It would be easy to blame Glover for not admitting that Horne and Jackson were upstairs. But Longarm and the two Kansas City coppers had suspected that anyway, so Glover's lie hadn't really changed anything. Longarm, Gibson, and Tinsley would have gone upstairs to search for the fugitives regardless of what Glover had said.

"Maybe you and Red Mike ought to think a mite harder about the hombres you rent rooms to," Longarm said as he clenched his teeth on the cheroot.

"I intend to. And there ain't no Red Mike, or any color Mike. This is my place. Fella who had it before me gave it that name."

Longarm grunted. He didn't care where the name had come from. All that mattered was that a good policeman had been hurt here . . . and that he had the tiniest of leads to Angela Boothe.

Sometimes, though, that was enough to put a man on the right trail.

The carpet runner had been taken up in the second-floor hallway at the Metrolite. The bloodstains where Stewart Winchell and Grace Dugan had died were just too large for the carpet to be salvaged, Longarm supposed. The whole thing would have to be replaced.

Parmenter offered to give Longarm another room, but the big lawman declined. It was possible that Sparling, Horne, and Jackson had had another partner who might come after him, but Longarm didn't think it was likely. Since all three of them were dead, he figured nobody else would try to ambush him, at least not tonight.

He wanted to stay close by where Winchell and Grace had died, too. That would keep the fires of anger and determination stoked inside him.

He didn't sleep well. He had seen the life go out of too many eyes in a short period of time, and the intimacy of those deaths bothered him. But he finally managed to doze off. He was up early the next morning, and after a quick breakfast in the hotel dining room that reminded him too much of the meals he had shared there with Winchell, he headed for the Western Union office down the street.

Longarm sent a telegram containing a few tersely worded questions to Billy Vail, then he walked over to the Union Pacific depot. After a few minutes he found himself in the office of the stationmaster, a balding man named Bradley.

"Sure, I knew Ted Sparling," Bradley said in reply to Longarm's question. "I heard he got himself killed last night."

"That he did," Longarm confirmed.

Bradley shook his head. "Well, I must say I'm not surprised. I always thought he would come to a bad end, hanging around with those ruffians like he did."

"Horne and Jackson?"

"Yes, I think that's them. Are they dead, too?"

Longarm nodded. "Dead as can be."

"Good riddance. I suspected that they robbed some of the travelers passing through Kansas City and that Sparling was tipping them off about which were the most likely victims. Never could prove it, though."

That sounded like something the three bushwhackers would have done, all right, Longarm thought. He said, "What job did Sparling have here?"

"Baggage and freight handler, mostly. If you ever saw him, you know he was a big, strong man. He could wrestle heavy crates around by himself. And when he wasn't drinking, he was willing to work; I'll give him credit for that much, anyway."

"So Sparling would have seen most everything that was loaded on the trains pulling out of here," Longarm said.

Bradley nodded. "During the times he was working, yes."

Longarm rolled a cheroot between his fingers. "Ever have trains come through at night?"

"Sure," the stationmaster said. "Quite often, in fact."

Longarm thought back and did some ciphering in his head. "You keep records of which trains go through and where they're bound?"

"Of course. We log everything that passes through this station."

"I need to see your records for, say, ten to fourteen days ago." That was the time period in which Angela Boothe had most likely disappeared from Kansas City.

Bradley looked puzzled, but he nodded his agreement. "If you want to wait right here, Marshal, I'll have my clerk get them out for you."

Longarm smoked the cheroot while he waited, then leaned forward to look at the logbook that Bradley spread open on the desk. He ran his finger along the entries that most interested him. Twelve days earlier, a westbound train had rolled out of the Kansas City station at 11:30 at night, heading for Santa Fe, in New Mexico Territory, and ultimately Los Angeles, out in California. That was the most likely one, in Longarm's opinion.

48

"What about passenger lists?" he asked. "You don't have a record of who bought tickets on a particular train, do you?"

Bradley shrugged his shoulders. "I'm afraid not, Marshal. Most tickets are sold for cash, and we don't know who we're selling them to."

Longarm pointed to the entry he had singled out. "Any way to know if Sparling was working that night?"

"Now, employee work records are something we do have. Let me look."

A few minutes later, Bradley confirmed that Ted Sparling had been working as a baggage and freight handler on the night in question. Longarm felt more sure than ever that he was on the right trail.

"I'm obliged," he said as he got to his feet. He shook hands with Bradley.

"If there's anything else we can do, Marshal, just let us know."

Longarm nodded and left the depot. By the time he got back to the Western Union office, he found a reply from Billy Vail waiting for him. The clerk slid the message flimsy through the wicket and across the counter. Longarm picked it up and read the words printed there in block letters.

TRIDENT RANCH NEAR SANTA FE OWNED BY GRANT
STOCKTON **STOP** STOCKTON VISITED KC TWO WEEKS
AGO **STOP** ANY LUCK VAIL

A grim smile tugged at Longarm's mouth under the sweeping mustaches. Luther Jackson hadn't said "stockman"; he had said "Stockton"—although it appeared that the man he'd been talking about was indeed a rancher. Longarm had put "try" and "dent" together to get "trident," and that had prompted his telegram to Billy Vail, asking the chief marshal to send wires to all the brand registries across the western states, asking if anyone owned the Trident brand. Longarm still wasn't sure about "gone to the devil," although he supposed the devil's pitchfork could also be called a trident. Taken all together, the evidence seemed to point to a connection between Angela Boothe's disappearance and Grant Stockton of New Mexico Territory.

So he supposed he would have to answer yes to Vail's question about whether or not he'd had any luck in his quest to find the missing woman. He was on Angela's trail.

But he would know more when he got to New Mexico.

# Chapter 9

The train rolled through Raton Pass, on the border between Colorado and New Mexico Territory. To the west loomed the Sangre de Christo Mountains, where quite a few of Longarm's cases had taken him. Up ahead in the valley below the pass was the rough frontier town of Raton, also a frequent destination. Today, though, Longarm was just passing through. He was bound for Santa Fe, and then the Trident Ranch belonging to Grant Stockton.

It had been nice to leave Kansas City behind, along with the ugly memories it held. As the train had rolled across the plains and then into the mountains, Longarm's mood had improved. He was still hungry for vengeance, though, on whoever was responsible for the deaths of Stewart Winchell and Grace Dugan. He would see justice done, no matter how long it took.

Night had fallen by the time the train reached Santa Fe. Despite being the territorial capital, the old town had a sleepy feeling to it. The streets were narrow and crooked, to the point that an old saying claimed they were laid out by a drunken Mexican on a blind mule. Many of the buildings dated from the time of Spanish rule and were quite impressive in their adobe architecture. There were missions in Santa Fe that were even older. Longarm liked the town and usually enjoyed visiting it.

Now, though, he was here on business, and he wasn't going to let himself get distracted. As soon as he stepped off the train carrying his lone bag, he headed for the sheriff's office.

A light still burned in the office window despite the lateness of the hour. Longarm turned the knob on the door and swung it open. A young man wearing a deputy's badge stood at the black cast-iron stove, pouring himself a cup of coffee from a battered old pot. He looked over his shoulder at Longarm and asked, "Can I help you, mister?"

"Sheriff in?"

"No, sir, he's gone down to Albuquerque on county business. Even if he hadn't, he wouldn't be here this time of night." The young deputy grinned. "He likes to have his supper and turn in early, the sheriff does. He left me in charge while he's gone. Name's Barry Quinn."

"Custis Long," Longarm introduced himself. "I'm a deputy, myself. Deputy U.S. marshal out of Denver."

Quinn looked impressed. "You're a federal lawman? Are you down here on a case, Marshal?"

"That's right," Longarm answered to both questions. He took out his badge and identification papers and showed them to the youngster, just so there wouldn't be any doubt about his identity. He went on, "I need some information, and if you've been in these parts for a while, maybe you can help me."

"Born and raised in New Mexico Territory," Quinn said. He hefted the coffeepot he was still holding. "Want some?"

Longarm nodded and said, "Much obliged."

They settled down with cups of coffee, Quinn behind the desk and Longarm in a chair in front of it. Longarm got right to the point. "I'm looking for a man named Grant

Stockton. He's supposed to own a ranch somewhere around here called the Trident."

Quinn nodded. "Sure, I know who Mr. Stockton is. His spread is northwest of here, along the Rio Grande not far from Los Alamos. Pretty big place. Used to be the X-Seven, until Mr. Stockton bought it and changed the brand."

"Rich man, is he?"

"He is," Quinn said. "Came from back east somewhere. Seemed to have plenty of money when he got here. He moved in and started expanding the spread right away."

"You know him personally?"

The deputy laughed. "We don't move in the same social circles, if that's what you mean, Marshal. Mr. Stockton's friends are all in high places. He travels around, and folks come to visit him at his ranch."

"But you know him when you see him?"

"Oh, sure," Quinn said with a wave of his hand. "Right handsome gent, I reckon. In his thirties, with lots of wavy brown hair. A lot of ladies set their caps for him, but he doesn't pay them much mind."

"So he's not married?"

"No, his sister lives with him. She's the hostess when they throw parties out at the ranch. He likes to have big ol' barbecues for his friends."

Quinn was a willing source of information, and he didn't seem the least bit curious about why Longarm wanted to know so much about Grant Stockton. Longarm asked, "Is Stockton at his ranch now?"

"I think so. He went to Kansas City a few weeks ago, but he's been back for a while."

"How do you know he went to Kansas City?"

"Oh, Mr. Stockton's friendly enough. He comes into town on business pretty often, and he talks to folks openly enough. People hereabouts generally like him." Quinn added casually, "You're not down here to cause trouble for him, are you, Marshal?"

"Nope," Longarm said. "He might have some information that would help me with a case I'm working on, that's all."

That was stretching the truth pretty thin, Longarm thought, but he wasn't ready to lay his cards on the table, even with a fellow lawman. For all he knew, Grant Stockton had kidnapped Angela Boothe and slipped her out of Kansas City with Ted Sparling's connivance, and until he had checked out that possibility he was going to play his cards close to the vest.

"I'd be glad to ride out there with you tomorrow and introduce you," Quinn offered.

Longarm shook his head. "Thanks, Deputy, but that won't be necessary. Just tell me how to find the place and I'll rent a horse and ride out on my own. No need for you to bother with it."

Quinn sipped his coffee and studied Longarm with a scrutiny that told the big lawman he wasn't quite as much of a naïve youngster as he seemed at first. "I reckon you'd rather I just keep this conversation between us?" he asked.

"That'd be best," Longarm said.

"All right. The sheriff always told me it's important for lawmen to cooperate with each other, so I'll keep quiet about your visit, Marshal." Quinn's voice hardened. "I don't want any trouble around here, though. When the sheriff gets back, I want to be able to tell him that things were nice and peaceful while he was gone."

"I'm not looking to start trouble," Longarm answered, honestly enough. He didn't want a big ruckus. He just wanted to locate Angela Boothe and find out who had hired those bushwhackers back in Kansas City. That was all.

Of course, if it took a ruckus to accomplish those goals, that would just be too bad. . . .

"What's the best livery stable in town?" he went on.

"Ashton and Clark have a barn right down the street. They'll give you a good horse and an honest deal. Tack, too, if you need it."

Longarm drank the last of his coffee and then stood up. "I'm mighty obliged, Deputy."

"If you turn up anything the sheriff's office needs to know about, you'll be in touch, won't you?"

"Sure," Longarm promised. "Like I said, I'm not looking for trouble. And I believe in lawmen cooperating with each other, too."

He walked across the plaza to a hotel where he had stayed before in Santa Fe. The clerk didn't remember him, and Longarm was glad of that. Until he found out what the connection was between Stockton and Angela Boothe, he planned to keep his true identity a secret. He signed the register as Custis Parker, a false name he used sometimes.

His room was on the second floor of the big, square adobe building. He stowed his gear, what little there was of it, ate a late supper in the hotel dining room, and then went back up to turn in. With the lamp turned low, he stripped down to the bottom half of a pair of long-handled underwear, then took a quart bottle of Tom Moore out of his bag. He swallowed a slug of the rye and put the cork back in the neck of the bottle. He planned to smoke a final cheroot before going to sleep, but he paused before lighting it as he heard a buggy or a wagon rattle by in the street outside.

Some instinct made him blow out the lamp and take a quick step over to the window. With the cheroot clenched between his teeth, he pulled the curtain back and looked out. The window was up a few inches to let in fresh air, which was why he had heard the vehicle passing by. It was a buggy, Longarm saw, and was being handled by one man. As the buggy turned a corner, Longarm got a

55

good look at the driver's profile in some light that spilled through the open doors of a saloon. The lawman's teeth bit down harder on the cheroot.

The driver wore a dark suit and a hat. He was unmistakably the same man who had mysteriously appeared in Kansas City, shot Bill Horne on the second floor of Red Mike's, and then just as mysteriously vanished.

Pierre Dushane.

# Chapter 10

The buggy finished turning the corner and was gone. Longarm leaned forward, his hands resting on the windowsill. He didn't have a horse or any other means of following Dushane, and if he ran downstairs in his balbriggans and gave chase on foot, Deputy Quinn might come along and haul him away to the hoosegow for creating a public disturbance. Longarm sighed in frustration.

Dushane was gone . . . for the moment. Based on everything that had happened, though, Longarm had a feeling that he might run into the little Frenchman again.

As he lay in the hotel bed trying to go to sleep, he thought over what he had learned about Grant Stockton. The man was an Easterner, and he was rich. He had come to New Mexico Territory and bought himself a ranch. Fellas like that sometimes thought that they were a law unto themselves, that their wealth and power and influence gave them the right to do whatever they wanted to. And more often than not, they got away with it.

Of course, the fact that Stockton was rich didn't have to mean that he was like that. Longarm had known plenty of rich men who were as solid and dependable as the earth itself, men like Charlie Goodnight over in the Texas panhandle and old "Jaggers" Dunn, the chairman of the Central Pacific Railroad. Longarm knew the scripture about the camel passing through the eye of a needle easier than a rich man could get into Heaven, but it wasn't *always* true.

Still, he was looking forward to meeting Mr. Grant Stockton. Longarm figured it would be mighty interesting. . . .

The next morning, Longarm visited the livery stable Deputy Quinn had recommended and rented a sorrel gelding with three white stockings. Normally he rode a McClellan saddle, but the livery didn't have one available so he rented a regular stock saddle instead. He had done considerable cowboying when he first came west after the Late Unpleasantness, so the presence of a saddle horn didn't bother him. It brought back memories of a lot of hot, dusty days and long, cold nights on the trail, though, from the time when he had choused herds of longhorns up from Texas through Indian Territory to the railheads in Kansas.

He was dressed cow today, having packed away his brown tweed suit, his vest, his white shirt, and his string tie. Now he wore denim trousers and a butternut shirt, and looked more like a drifting puncher than a lawman. One of the proprietors of the livery stable looked at him and said, "Huh. That's a mite odd, a cowboy without a horse."

"Lost him up the other side of Raton," Longarm extemporized. "He stepped in a hole and busted his leg. I had to carry my saddle in, and then I sold it so I could buy a train ticket down here."

"You must've wanted to get to Santa Fe real bad, mister."

"I heard there's work to be had on the Trident spread. I had a little money left over, so I decided to rent a horse and take a *paseo* out there. If I can get a riding job, maybe the boss will front me enough money to buy that sorrel."

"He might. Mr. Stockton's a generous man."

Quinn had mentioned that Stockton was well liked in the area. Spreading around plenty of money was one way to accomplish that.

Longarm rode out of Santa Fe, following the directions the deputy had given him the night before. A fairly good road led from the town to Stockton's Trident Ranch, and it was easy to find. The Rio Grande was about thirty miles to the west, and beyond it rose the rugged peaks of the Sierra Nacimiento range. On this side of the great river were smaller foothills with broad, lush-grassed valleys between them. It was good rangeland for a man strong enough to take and keep it, and evidently Grant Stockton was.

Being in the saddle again felt good to Longarm. As he jogged along under blue, cloud-dotted skies, he thought about how he would approach Stockton. If the rancher was responsible for Angela Boothe's disappearance, waltzing onto the Trident, announcing his identity, and asking a lot of questions probably wouldn't get Longarm anything except some hot lead answers. On the other hand, if he could get a job on the place, as he had told the liveryman, that would give him a chance to do some discreet poking around. That seemed to be the best approach.

The hour was nearing the middle of the day when he rode around a bend in the trail and reined in abruptly at the sight of someone lying on the ground up ahead. Longarm frowned as he studied the huddled shape. The person's back was to him, but the way those denim trousers hugged their wearer's hips was decidedly unmasculine. The head sported a mass of thick, wavy brown hair. Longarm knew that he was looking at a woman.

But she wasn't moving, which meant she was either hurt and unconscious . . . or dead.

A saddled horse stood about fifty yards away, cropping contentedly at the grass. The sight of the riderless animal gave Longarm a pretty good idea what had happened. The horse had spooked for some reason and pitched off its rider. The woman had fallen and likely knocked herself out when she landed. At least, Longarm hoped that was the extent of it. He heeled the sorrel into motion and rode forward.

When he reached the woman he swung down from the saddle and quickly knelt beside her. Putting a hand on her shoulder, he rolled her gently onto her back. As her face came into view, he saw that she was young, no more than twenty-five, and other than the fact that she was pale and had a goose egg on her forehead where she had hit it on something, she was beautiful. She wore a man's shirt that was tight over her breasts, and as Longarm looked at them, he saw that they rose and fell regularly. The woman was alive and probably not hurt too badly. He figured she had been tossed off her horse only a few minutes earlier and would probably be coming around any time now.

In fact, her eyelids were already starting to flutter. After a moment she opened them, revealing blue eyes that looked both hurt and confused. She started to sit up, saying, "Wh-what . . . who . . ."

Longarm put a hand on her shoulder. He saw her eyes roll up and knew that she had been struck by a wave of dizziness. He slipped an arm under her shoulders to keep her from falling back.

"Take it easy," he told her. "You're all right, ma'am. Just don't go to moving around too much or too fast for a few minutes."

She closed her eyes and took several deep breaths to steady herself. When she looked up at him again, she was able to ask in a reasonably coherent tone, "Who are you, sir?"

"Name's Parker, ma'am," Longarm told her, "Custis

Parker. I was just riding along and saw you lying here. I figured you'd been throwed."

"That's right, I was. My horse . . . my horse saw a rattlesnake and got frightened." She turned her head to look around. "The snake—"

"I don't see a rattler anywhere around here, ma'am," Longarm assured her. "I imagine he was just as spooked as your horse was and crawled off as soon as he got the chance."

The woman sighed. "I hope so. I hate snakes." She paused, then went on, "I think I can sit up now. I can't expect you to kneel here holding me all day."

Longarm grinned and said, "I can think of worse ways to spend some time. I'll help you sit up, though. Just take it slow and easy."

After a moment, the young woman was sitting up by herself on the trail. Longarm hunkered on his heels beside her. "Are you sure you're all right?" he asked. "That rattler didn't bite you before he slithered off, did he?"

"No, I think I'm fine. I just hit my head when I landed, and it knocked me silly for a few minutes."

"No offense, ma'am, but you weren't knocked silly. You were out cold when I got here."

"Yes, I suppose I was. After hearing that rattle and having my horse rear up, I don't remember anything until . . . well, until I woke up and saw you, Mr. Parker. Thank you for helping me."

"I didn't do much," Longarm said. "You would've come to whether I came along or not."

"Yes, but just having you here made it easier. I wasn't as frightened this way." She looked around. "I think I'd like to stand up now."

"Sure. Just—"

"Take it slow and easy, I know."

Longarm came to his feet. He reached down and took her hands when she held them up to him. He lifted her, and as she came upright, another dizzy spell evidently hit her. She said, "Oh!" and stumbled toward him.

Longarm put his arms around her to steady her. She leaned against him and said, "Oh, my God. I'm sorry, Mr. Parker. I know this is terribly bold behavior, but I'd rather have you hold me than fall on my face again."

"You go right ahead and let your head settle down, ma'am. Probably won't take more'n a minute or two."

Those were certainly pleasurable minutes, Longarm thought. The woman's head came up about to his chin, which meant he didn't have any trouble smelling the clean scent of her thick brown hair. Her breasts rested comfortably against him, soft and round and warm in the man's shirt she wore. The embrace they shared was almost as close as that of two lovers. Almost, but not quite.

Near enough to make his manhood perk up and take notice, though. It might be better for her to step away before she felt it prodding the softness of her belly.

However, she didn't seem to be in any hurry to move out of his arms. "I'm feeling better now," she said in a soft voice, "but I think you'd better hold me for a little while longer, just to make sure I'm all right."

"I reckon I can do that, Miss . . . ?"

"Stockton," she said. "Marie Stockton. This is my brother's range we're on."

This was a stroke of luck, Longarm thought. . . .

And then a moment later, he began to wonder if he was so lucky after all, when a loud, angry voice yelled, "Unhand that woman, *mein Herr,* or I shall blast your brains all over the ground!"

# Chapter 11

Longarm had met German fellas before, so he recognized the accent. When he turned his head to look over his shoulder, he saw a stocky, red-faced gent striding toward him, carrying a shotgun. The man wore high black boots, whipcord trousers, a leather hunting jacket, and a narrow-brimmed hat with a feather stuck in the band. The getup looked a mite ridiculous in these surroundings, but there was nothing funny about the scattergun in his hands.

"Better lower that greener, old son," Longarm advised the stranger. "If it goes off, you're liable to kill both me and the lady."

"Please do as Mr. Parker says, Count," Marie Stockton added hurriedly. "I'm all right, I assure you."

The German looked doubtful. "But *Fräulein,* I come along to find this . . . cowboy mauling you!"

"He was just helping me to my feet," Marie explained. "I'm a little dizzy, because my horse threw me and I hit my head when I fell."

The twin barrels of the shotgun lowered slightly. "You are certain about this, *Fräulein?*"

"I think I know what happened," Marie said crisply. "Now, please, Count, lower that gun."

63

"Yah, yah." The stocky German let the scattergun all the way down, so that the barrels pointed at the ground. He had a monocle attached to a ribbon on the lapel of his jacket. He picked up the eyepiece and screwed it into the socket of his right eye, squinting through the glass at Longarm. "You should step away from this man. He has an evil look about him."

"I'm harmless, old son," Longarm said. To prove it, he stepped back, putting a little distance between himself and Marie Stockton. He felt a little pang of disappointment as her lithe, warm body slipped out of his arms, but it couldn't be helped. He had a role to play, a pose as a drifting cowboy to maintain.

"And I really am grateful to him for his help," Marie added. She made a formal introduction. "Count von Steglitz, this is Mr. Custis Parker. Mr. Parker, Count Otto von Steglitz."

The count practically clicked the heels of his boots together. He was one of those Prussians, Longarm thought, with a stiff-necked military bearing bred into his blood. Longarm gave him a casual nod and said, "Pleased to meet you, Count."

"Likewise, a pleasure to make your acquaintance, sir," von Steglitz said, but didn't really sound too happy about it.

"The count is a guest of my brother's and mine," Marie explained. "He's come to see the American West."

"Yah, and a magnificent country it is, too." Von Steglitz opened his eye wider and let the monocle drop to his chest on its ribbon. "You know it well, *Herr* Parker?"

"I've traveled over a heap of it," Longarm said.

Before he could go on, the rataplan of approaching hoofbeats interrupted him. Several riders swept around a nearby bend in the trail and then reined in sharply as they saw Longarm, Marie Stockton, and the count standing there.

The man in the lead was dressed in range clothes, but they looked new and hardly broken in, telling Longarm that the hombre wasn't in the habit of doing a lot of work in them. He was in his thirties, well built and handsome, and when he cuffed his cream-colored Stetson back on his head, he revealed a lot of thick, wavy brown hair. He matched the description of Grant Stockton that Deputy Quinn had given Longarm.

Three men and a woman were with him. One of the men was obviously a working cowboy, probably one of the hands from the Trident. The other two men and the woman were Easterners. Longarm could tell that by looking at them, even though they, like the man he took to be Stockton, wore range clothes. The butt of a Winchester stuck up from a saddle boot on Stockton's horse, and he reached for it as he said, "Marie? Are you all right? What's going on here?"

"Do not worry, *Herr* Stockton," the count said before Marie could reply. "I have assured myself that your lovely sister is quite safe. She is under my protection."

"I don't need protecting," Marie said. "I wasn't in any danger except from the rattlesnake."

The woman with Stockton said shrilly, "Rattlesnake? Oh, my God. There are rattlesnakes out here?" She turned to the rider beside her. "Timothy, what sort of terrible place have you brought me to?"

"Don't get so upset about a little snake," the man said, impatience and irritation in his voice. "You're not in any danger, Millie."

The woman sniffed. "I've told you not to call me that. My name is Millicent."

"I know your name. I married you, didn't I?"

They were young, about Marie Stockton's age. The woman, with dark hair, olive skin, and flashing eyes, was very attractive, but Longarm had a feeling she was a spoiled brat most of the time. Her husband had a handsome but dim-witted look about him.

The final member of the little group was middle-aged and had a cigar in his mouth. He took a bandanna from his pocket, removed his hat, and used the bandanna to mop sweat from a mostly bald head with only a fringe of reddish gray hair remaining around the ears. Unlike the young couple, he had a hard, competent look about him.

Stockton edged his horse forward and asked again, "What happened here, Marie?"

"A snake spooked my horse, and I fell off," she explained for the third time. "I hit my head and knocked myself out. Mr. Parker here came along just before I regained consciousness and helped me."

Stockton swung down from the saddle and stepped quickly to his sister's side to examine the swelling on her forehead. "You're going to have a bruise there," he said after a moment.

"It'll heal," Marie told him. "You're sweet to be so concerned about me, Grant, but really, I'm all right."

"Of course I'm concerned about you. You're my sister." Stockton's voice held gruff affection. He turned to Longarm. "Your name is Parker?"

Longarm held out a hand. "Custis Parker."

Without hesitation, Stockton shook with him, and the rancher's grip was firm. "I'm Grant Stockton. This is my spread, the Trident."

Longarm nodded. "I heard about your ranch down in Santa Fe, Mr. Stockton. In fact, that's why I rode out here. I was hoping you might have a riding job for a good hand."

"I'm always looking for good men, but you'll have to talk to my foreman, Ben Harwell." Stockton jerked his head toward the puncher who rode with them.

The man sidled his horse forward and cast an appraising eye at Longarm. Like most ranch ramrods Longarm had come across, Harwell seemed able to size up a man just by looking at him. After a moment, the thick-mustached foreman nodded and said, "I reckon there's a chance he'll do, Mr. Stockton. I'll want to jaw with him a while back at headquarters, though, before I make up my mind for sure. Only thing I'm worried about is that that's a livery stable horse. I recognize it from town."

"Had to shoot my horse a ways back," Longarm drawled. "Busted its leg in a hole. I sold my saddle and scraped up enough dinero to get to Santa Fe and rent this horse and rig."

Harwell frowned. "You sold your saddle? What the hell kind of a man would do a thing like that?"

Longarm tensed. A fella who was worth his salt wouldn't take that kind of talk, even from a man he was hoping to impress enough to hire him. "I didn't have any choice unless I wanted to hoof it from Raton to Santa Fe, and I'm damned if I'll walk that far. . . . Pardon my French, ladies."

Harwell frowned and said, "We'll talk about it."

"At the very least," Stockton said, "you'll come back to headquarters with us and have dinner. If my sister says you gave her a hand, that puts me in your debt."

"A fella would do as much for any woman." Longarm flashed a quick grin at Marie. "Especially one as pretty as Miss Stockton here."

"That'll be enough of that," Stockton said as Marie blushed, which made her even prettier.

"I'm sure Mr. Parker meant no offense," she said.

Stockton looked at von Steglitz. "What's your part in all this, Count?"

"I was riding along when I discovered your sister in the arms of this cowboy," von Steglitz said.

"I told you, he helped me up," Marie put in.

"Yah, that is what you said, *Fräulein.*" Von Steglitz's

tone made it clear he wasn't sure whether he believed her or not.

Stockton said firmly, "If that's what Marie says, then I'm sure she's right. Let's all get mounted up and head back." He smiled at the dark-haired young woman. "I'm sure Millicent would rather not risk running into any rattlesnakes."

Millicent shuddered daintily.

"I will fetch my mount," von Steglitz said. "I left him concealed in the bushes."

Longarm caught the reins of Marie's horse and led the animal over to her. "Thank you," she said as she took the reins from him, and he noticed that her fingers brushed his for a second longer than was absolutely necessary. He had been instantly attracted to her, and it looked as if the feeling was mutual.

When von Steglitz had rejoined them and the whole party was mounted and riding toward the Trident Ranch headquarters, Stockton introduced Longarm to the other members of the group. "Timothy Ford and his wife, Millicent," the rancher said, nodding toward the young couple. "And this is Jason Lawlor."

Lawlor was the bald-headed man. He reached over and shook with Longarm. His hand was dry and strong. "Good to meet you, Parker," he said.

"Jason is a business associate of mine from back east," Stockton explained, "and Timothy and Millicent are friends of the family."

"You do business with the count as well?" Longarm asked.

"His family owns one of the largest shipping lines in Europe. Before I moved out here to New Mexico and became a cattleman, we were involved in many deals together." Stockton added, "Not that it's any of your business, Mr. Parker."

"No, it sure ain't," Longarm agreed. "No offense meant."

"None taken. What's your line of work, Mr. Parker? Oh, that's right, you're a cowboy."

Longarm smiled faintly. "I've seen the hind end of more cows than I like to think about."

Ben Harwell moved in close on Longarm's other side. "Who have you ridden for?"

Longarm named several spreads he had actually worked for back in his cowboying days and added a few more well-known ranches owned by men who were his friends. Harwell warmed up to him a little more after that. It was an impressive cow-country pedigree.

Marie Stockton spoke to Longarm a few times during the ride, too, but protective glances from her brother made her keep a discreet distance most of the time. That was all right, Longarm thought. If he got a job on the Trident as he hoped, he would have other chances to spend time with Marie Stockton. Right now it was more important that he put himself in position to find a lead to the whereabouts of the missing Angela Boothe.

The Trident was a fine spread; Longarm could tell that from the pastureland they rode through and the fat, healthy cattle grazing in those pastures. After a while they came to a rise that overlooked the valley of the Rio Grande, with the rugged mountains on the far side. The main ranch house was located on top of the rise, a sprawling, two-story dwelling made of thick logs. A cook shack, a smokehouse, a long bunkhouse, a blacksmith shop, several barns, and a large network of corrals were all nearby. Everything about it radiated wealth and success.

A wide, roofed gallery ran around three sides of the ranch house. Several people sat in rocking chairs on the gallery. More guests of Stockton's, Longarm thought. Probably rich folks from back east. Stockton rode straight to the house and dismounted, as did the others. Longarm followed suit. Cowboys came from one of the barns to take the horses. Along with Ben Harwell, they led the animals away. Harwell said over his shoulder to Longarm, "Come on out to the bunkhouse after dinner, Parker, and we'll palaver more."

Longarm nodded. He turned toward the gallery as Stockton bounded up the steps and greeted a short, buxom, young blond woman who stood up from one of the rocking chairs and came toward him with her hands outstretched. Longarm looked at the woman and tried to keep his face impassive as he realized that she matched the description he had been given of Angela Boothe. Surely, he thought, he couldn't be that lucky.

That was before Grant Stockton took the woman's hands, leaned forward to kiss her on the cheek, and said, "Angela, my dear, how are you?"

# Chapter 12

Longarm thought he'd managed to keep the surprise off his face. It took even more of an effort a moment later, after the woman replied in a sleepy voice that she was fine, when Stockton turned to Longarm and said, "Parker, this is another friend of mine, Miss Angela Boothe."

Reaching up to tug politely on the brim of his Stetson, Longarm nodded and said, "I'm mighty pleased to meet you, ma'am."

Angela Boothe couldn't know just how true that statement was.

She was as pretty as she had been described to Longarm, with a rounded face and long, straight blond hair that hung down her back almost to her waist. Her body had lush curves in all the right places. She gave Longarm only a brief, disinterested smile, though, before turning her attention back to Stockton. "When are we leaving?" she asked, a slight whine in her voice. Like Millicent Ford, she seemed quite spoiled.

Stockton chuckled. "Be patient, my dear, be patient. The rest of our journey will begin soon enough."

Longarm didn't like the sound of that.

He was thinking fast, trying to come to grips with this

71

unexpected discovery. As he had suspected, Angela Boothe had left Kansas City with Grant Stockton. She was standing right there on the gallery, living proof of that theory. Longarm had thought that she had been kidnapped, though, and from the way she was billing and cooing at Stockton, that was clearly wrong. From all appearances, Angela had come with the cattleman of her own free will. Obviously, she planned on going somewhere else with him, too.

But if there was nothing suspicious about her departure from Kansas City, why hadn't she wired her aunt and uncle about where she was going, as had been her habit up to that point in her visit to America? More importantly, why had Stockton hired those three toughs, Sparling, Horne, and Jackson, to kill anybody who came looking for her? Longarm was still convinced that was what had happened. Stockton had tried to cover up Angela's trail, and that had led to the murders of Grace Dugan and Stewart Winchell. The rancher had a lot to answer for.

So in a way, Longarm had done his job—there was Angela Boothe in the flesh, standing on the gallery holding Stockton's hands—but there were still too many questions yet to be answered, too many rocks to turn over to see what would scurry out from underneath. Longarm decided he was going to continue his pose as a drifting cowhand and see what he could find out.

The other two people on the gallery were a middle-aged couple, Edward and Claire Wilcox. Stockton introduced them to Longarm as everyone went inside the big house. Like the others, the Wilcoxes were Easterners and gave off an air of being well-to-do and quite satisfied with themselves. Longarm didn't care much for any of the people he had met this morning, with the exceptions of Marie Stockton and Ben Harwell. Marie seemed level-headed and more down to earth than the others, and Harwell, despite his curt manner, was a Westerner through and through, as solid as an old oak tree.

The big living room into which Stockton led the group was expensively and comfortably furnished, with heavy divans and chairs scattered around, thick rugs on the floor, a massive stone fireplace on one side, and colorful, intricately woven Navajo rugs hung on the walls. The fireplace had a huge spread of longhorns over it. A gun cabinet with a latticed front held more than a dozen fine rifles and shotguns.

Stockton went to a small, highly polished bar and said, "It's after noon, I believe. What would everyone like to drink?"

"I want some of that brandy," Angela Boothe said without hesitation. "I haven't had any since that little bit in my coffee this morning."

Judging from her heavy-lidded eyes and slightly slurred voice, she'd had more than a little dollop in her coffee, Longarm thought. But Stockton just smiled and poured some liquor from a crystal decanter into an equally fancy snifter and held it out to her. Angela took it, sipped the fiery stuff, and smiled in satisfaction.

Longarm noticed that Stockton corked the decanter and put it away under the counter as soon as he had poured Angela's drink, not offering the brandy to anyone else. Not that anyone asked for it. Stockton's private bar had a better selection of spirits than some saloons Longarm had been in. The guests gathered around, with Stockton playing the gracious host.

Longarm hung back, though, and so did Marie. "I'm not sure I should have anything to drink after hitting my head that way," she said.

"That's probably a good idea," Longarm told her. "Sometimes folks who get walloped like that think they're all right, but they really ain't."

"I'm reasonably confident I didn't do any permanent

damage, but I'd rather be on the safe side." She smiled at him and slid her arm through his. "Come with me, Mr. Parker, while my brother is busy with his guests."

She steered him out of the main room and down a hall to a large room that was lined with bookshelves. The shelves were filled with thick, leather-bound volumes. The writing on the spines was so faded with time that he couldn't read most of the titles or authors. The ones he could read were foreign-sounding names that weren't familiar to him, like Alhazred and Von Junzt. He was a little surprised not to see a copy of *Ben-Hur,* the new novel by General Lew Wallace, who was the governor of New Mexico Territory. Seemed like just about every household in the country had a copy of that book, along with the Bible.

Come to think of it, he didn't see a Bible anywhere on the shelves, either.

Marie went to a large desk and sat down behind it. Longarm perched a hip on one corner of the desk and leaned there with his Stetson in his hand.

"Even though my brother considers this his sanctum sanctorum, I retreat in here sometimes when the chattering gets too loud and annoying."

"You don't like your brother's friends?"

"I suppose they're all right. The count is a bit of a lech. Timothy and Millicent squabble all the time, and to be honest, neither of them is very bright. The Wilcoxes are just plain stuffy."

"What about Miss Boothe?"

Marie cocked an eyebrow. "Grant has grown very fond of her in a short period of time."

"Where did they meet?"

"In Kansas City. Grant was there on business, and he brought her back to the ranch with him."

"You didn't go along on the trip?" Longarm asked.

"No. Grant tends to all the business in the family. I'm

here strictly as a hostess, and for decorative purposes."

Longarm could tell she resented being regarded like that. He said, "Well, begging your pardon, ma'am, but you are mighty decorative. I think a fella would be foolish not to see that there's a lot more to you than that, though."

Marie smiled. "You're kind, Mr. Parker."

"Call me Custis."

"Custis," she repeated. "That's an odd name. It suits you, though."

"Because I'm odd?" Longarm asked with a grin.

"Not at all. It's a strong name, and you're a strong man." She blushed slightly. "I know that from experience."

"I never meant to be too bold, out there on the trail—"

"You weren't too bold at all, Custis," she said. "In fact, if the count hadn't come along, you could have been even more bold and it would have been all right with me."

Longarm chuckled. "You say what you mean, don't you, ma'am?"

"And I mean what I say," Marie responded solemnly.

Longarm steered the conversation back to safer ground. "What about Jason Lawlor?" he asked. "You didn't mention him."

"I don't really know much about him. He's another business associate of Grant's, but he's not like the others. He's much more serious. Almost . . . frightening, in a way."

Longarm hadn't found Jason Lawlor particularly frightening, but he knew what Marie meant about him being different from the others.

"Miss Boothe's the one who interests me," Longarm ventured.

Marie arched her eyebrows this time. "Is that so? I suppose I can understand why. She's very pretty. And she's English, which I suppose makes her . . . I don't know, an exotic foreigner."

Longarm shook his head. "That ain't really it. From the looks of it, she's mighty fond of that brandy your brother was doling out."

"I'm not sure her drinking habits are any of our business," Marie said, her voice cool now, and Longarm thought he might have overplayed his hand a little.

Before he could say anything else, footsteps sounded in the hallway, and Grant Stockton put his head into the room. "There you are!" he said, not sounding particularly happy about it. "I wondered where the two of you had gotten off to. Come along now, dinner is ready." He stood there until Longarm and Marie both left the library and went toward the dining room.

When they entered the room, Longarm saw that it was dominated by a long mahogany table draped with a snowy white cloth and set with fine china and silverware. Indian women who were clearly servants brought platters of food from the kitchen and placed them on the table. Stockton's guests were taking their seats, with the exception of Count von Steglitz, who had pleaded a headache and gone upstairs to lie down. The rancher's place was at the head of the table, with his sister to his right and Angela Boothe to his left. Marie linked her arm with the big lawman's and made sure he was seated beside her. That put Jason Lawlor on Longarm's right. Timothy Ford sat across from Longarm, with his wife, Millicent, to his left. Claire Wilcox was to Lawlor's right, and Edward Wilcox sat at the far end. The only vacant seat at the table was next to Millicent and across from Claire. It was set with china and silver and a crystal wineglass, like the other places, and Longarm wondered if there was another guest on the Trident.

A moment later, he saw that there was, as a man bustled into the dining room from a different hallway. From the head of the table, Grant Stockton greeted him by saying, "I was afraid you weren't going to be able to join us, *M'sieur* Delacroix."

Once again, Longarm had to put an effort into keeping the surprise he felt from showing on his face. Stockton might have called the diminutive Frenchman Delacroix, but Longarm knew him by another name.

Pierre Dushane.

# Chapter 13

Dushane's mild blue eyes touched on Longarm only for an instant and seemed to pass over him without really noticing him. Longarm knew better, though. For days now, everywhere he went Dushane seemed to pop up sooner or later, so he supposed he shouldn't have been surprised to see the Frenchman here.

Dushane smiled at his host and said, "I would not miss an opportunity to avail myself of your most gracious hospitality, *M'sieur* Stockton." He moved to take the lone empty seat at the table.

"I don't believe you've met Mr. Parker," Stockton said.

Dushane looked at Longarm again, finally deigning to pay attention to him. "No, I do not believe that I have," he murmured.

Longarm stood up and reached across the table, offering with a blunt American informality to shake hands. "Custis Parker," he introduced himself. "Pleased to meet you, Mr. . . . ?"

"Delacroix. Henri Delacroix. And the pleasure is mine, *M'sieur* Parker."

Dushane's hand was small and soft, but his grip had some strength in it. He was putting on an act just like

Longarm was. They had gotten a good look at each other through the gunsmoke in the second-floor corridor of Red Mike's, back in Kansas City. Dushane might not know that the tall, rangy cowboy with the longhorn mustaches was actually a federal lawman, but he had to be aware that Longarm had been mixed up somehow with Horne and Jackson, and by association, with Stockton and Angela.

"You are another rancher, perhaps?" Dushane went on. He took his seat. "A neighbor of *M'sieur* Stockton's?"

"Nope, I'm just a cowboy riding the grub line," Longarm replied as he sat back down.

"Parker gave Marie a hand when her horse threw her this morning," Stockton explained.

Dushane looked at Marie and exclaimed, "*Mais non,* but you are not injured, *mademoiselle?* Name of a name, if any harm were to come to such a lovely, delicate flower—"

"I'm fine," Marie interrupted before Dushane could continue. "I just got a bump on my head. I wasn't in any real danger." She laid her right hand on top of Longarm's left. "But I appreciate Mr. Parker's help anyway, and I'm certainly glad he came along when he did."

"*Oui,* it was a fortuitous accident indeed," Dushane agreed.

"Not totally an accident," Stockton put in. "Parker was on his way out here to see about getting a job on the Trident."

Dushane nodded. "I see. And you are going to employ him?"

"I'm thinking about it." Stockton took a sip of wine from his glass and regarded Longarm intently. "I'm wondering, though, whether I really need another hand here on the ranch."

Longarm didn't like the sound of that. Stockton might feed him, then send him on his way and consider the debt squared for anything Longarm might have done for Marie.

"We'll discuss it later," Stockton went on. "Right now, let's just enjoy this excellent meal the servants have prepared."

Everyone dug in. The food was Mexican for the most part, tamales and tortillas and beans and peppers and chunks of lean steak. Longarm enjoyed it, although he noticed that some of the Easterners sort of picked at the food as if they weren't quite certain what it was. Not Marie, though. She ate heartily, and Longarm liked her even more for that. He didn't have much use for dainty women who ate like birds.

Dushane packed the grub away, too, especially considering that he was a little fella. That didn't affect his appetite, though.

Between bites, Longarm asked Dushane, "What's your line of work, Mr. Delacroix?"

"The law, *M'sieur* Parker. I am an attorney."

"Henri's a friend of a friend," Stockton said. "A fellow I do business with in Paris asked him to look me up while he was over here touring the States."

Dushane inclined his head. "And you have made me more than welcome, *mon ami.*"

For all Longarm knew, Dushane really was a lawyer, but he figured that friend-of-a-friend business was a pack of lies. Dushane had followed Stockton out here because he had gotten on Angela Boothe's trail the same way Longarm had. Somehow, Dushane had gotten ahead of Longarm and reached the Trident first. Longarm hadn't known it was going to be a race, or he would have tried to move a mite faster.

When the meal was over, everyone stood up and moved back into the big living room. Stockton kissed Angela on the forehead and said, "You look a bit tired, my dear. Why don't you go lie down for a while?"

She nodded and said, "Yes, I believe I'll do that. You're so considerate, Grant."

"I'm going upstairs, too," Millicent Ford announced. "It was a trying morning, all that talk of snakes."

Her husband, Timothy, helped himself to a drink, pouring a glass nearly full of whiskey before he slumped down in an armchair. He looked like he was settling in to get good and drunk, Longarm thought. Jason Lawlor went upstairs as well, muttering something about some correspondence he needed to catch up on. Edward and Claire Wilcox resumed their seats on the gallery. Claire took some needlework from a bag while Edward fired up a fat cigar.

That left Longarm, Stockton, Marie, and Dushane to find something to do. Stockton took care of that by saying to his sister, "Marie, darling, why don't you play some tunes on the harpsichord for *M'sieur* Delacroix? I'm sure such a refined gentleman as he is must think we're totally lacking in culture out here in the West."

Dushane waved one of those small hands. "But no, *m'sieur,* I am certain there is much refinement to be found in your country."

Stockton laughed and said, "Not to speak of, not in New Mexico Territory, anyway. Go ahead, Marie, play for our guest while Parker and I go out and talk to Ben Harwell for a while."

"Of course," Marie said, although she didn't look all that pleased by the idea.

Stockton took Longarm's elbow. "Come on, Parker."

Longarm tried not to bristle. Like most frontiersman, he didn't like to have hands laid on him, but Stockton probably didn't know that.

They walked out to the bunkhouse and found Harwell in a small office attached to the main building. The foreman said, "Come on in, boss. Have a seat."

Harwell had a pipe going. He puffed on it as Stockton

took out a thin black cigarillo and offered it to Longarm, who took it and nodded his thanks. He liked his three-for-a-nickel cheroots better, he reflected as he lit the smoke, but he was trying to be polite.

Stockton lit a cigarillo of his own and then said, "Tell us about those spreads you rode for, Parker." His tone now was that of a man talking to a prospective employee, not a host talking to a guest.

Longarm sat back, cocked his right ankle on his left knee, and spun a web of truths, half-truths, and outright lies. If Stockton and Harwell checked up on him, even the ranchers Longarm had never worked for would be glad to back up anything that "Custis Parker" said. All of them knew Longarm and knew that he sometimes used that alias while he was working undercover.

Finally, Harwell nodded and said, "I reckon you'll do, Parker. We can hire him on if you want, Mr. Stockton."

"Do we really *need* another hand right now, Ben?" Stockton asked.

The foreman looked a little uncomfortable. "Well, I can't say as we really do. We've got a good crew already. But we can make a place and find some work—"

"I don't think Mr. Parker here is the sort of man who would be satisfied with make-work," Stockton said. "He's too proud to accept charity. Aren't you, Parker?"

"I'm not looking for a handout, if that's what you mean." Longarm's voice was taut with anger, just as it should have been under the circumstances. "I rode out here to see about a job, but if there ain't a real one, that's just the way it is."

"Of course, you did help my sister . . ."

"And she said thanks. That's enough for me." Longarm came to his feet. "Reckon I'll be riding now."

Abruptly, Stockton grinned up at him and said, "Sit down, Parker, and don't get your dander up. No one asked you to leave. Just because I don't have a riding job for you doesn't mean that we can't do business."

Longarm frowned, but after a moment he sat down again. "What do you have in mind?" he asked.

Stockton nodded toward the Colt in the crossdraw rig on Longarm's left hip and asked, "Can you use that gun?"

"I don't take all day to haul it out, and I generally hit what I aim at, if that's what you mean."

"That's exactly what I mean." Stockton rolled the half-smoked cigarillo between his fingers. "I do want to hire you, Parker . . . you and your gun."

# Chapter 14

Longarm met Stockton's gaze squarely and said, "I'm not a hired killer."

"And I'm not asking you to be," Stockton said. "I'm not looking for an assassin. What I have in mind is more of a bodyguard."

"You want me to protect somebody?" Longarm asked.

"Several somebodies. You see, my sister and my friends and I—everyone you've met so far on the Trident, in fact, with the exception of Ben here—are about to leave for a trip to California. We're going by train, so it'll only take a few days, but I'd like to have a tough, competent man along with us just in case of trouble."

"Sounds to me like you're *expecting* trouble," Longarm said.

"You've probably figured out by now that I'm a fairly wealthy man."

"I sort of got that idea," Longarm said dryly.

"A man doesn't achieve the level of success in life that I have without making some enemies," Stockton said, a hard edge creeping into his voice. "There are men who are jealous of me, men who would like nothing better than

84

to destroy me. These men also would not hesitate to strike at me through my family or my friends."

"So you want somebody to protect you while you're on this trip to California," Longarm said.

"Don't think that I'm incapable of protecting myself," Stockton snapped. "I can handle a gun quite proficiently. But my enemies—one man in particular I'm thinking of— can afford to hire many guns. Have you ever heard of a man named Lucius Thorne?"

The question came quick and sharp, and Longarm knew Stockton was watching him intently for any sign of a lie. But he answered completely honestly as he said, "Nope, never heard of the gent."

"He's no gentleman, let me tell you that," Stockton said. "He's a cutthroat, nothing but a pirate in a suit. To be honest, Parker, I wondered a little if Thorne had sent you here to worm your way into my confidence and then betray me."

Longarm shook his head. "Like I said, I don't know the fella."

"And I believe you. I consider myself a good judge of character. I think you're an honest man, and that's what I need. Are you up for a trip west?"

Longarm shrugged. "As long as the wages are fair."

"Oh, I'll be more than generous, I assure you. We have a deal, then?" Stockton thrust out his hand.

Longarm took it and shook. "I reckon."

Harwell spoke up then, saying, "Boss, how do you know this fella can handle himself in case of trouble? You're just takin' his word for it." The foreman glanced at Longarm and added, "No offense, Parker."

"None taken," Longarm said. "You boys don't know me or what I can do. It's a good question."

Stockton smiled. "Well, if we do run into any of Thorne's men, at least you won't cost me anything if you can't live up to your claims, Parker." He put the cigarillo back in his mouth and clenched his teeth on it. "Because more than likely, they'll kill you."

A lot of things had happened in a fairly short period of time, the most important one being that Longarm had found Angela Boothe. But she hadn't been kidnapped and wasn't in any danger that he could see. However, he couldn't shake the feeling that something was wrong on the Trident spread, and his natural curiosity, as always, was both a blessing and a curse. He had to find out what was going on before he would feel comfortable getting in touch with Billy Vail. He still wanted answers to all his questions.

He would play out the string a while longer, he decided.

Grant Stockton, his sister, and all his guests would be taking the westbound train from Santa Fe in two days. That gave Longarm a little time to poke around the ranch. That first afternoon, he couldn't shake Ben Harwell. The foreman insisted on giving him a tour of the spread. "Who knows?" Harwell said. "Maybe when you get back from that trip to California, you'll be workin' on the place after all."

"Could be," Longarm agreed, since he couldn't very well say that he hoped to have the case completely wrapped up well before then.

The Trident was a fine spread, just as Longarm had thought from his earlier observations. Harwell had worked there ever since it was the X7.

"Mr. Stockton is from back east somewhere, ain't he?" Longarm said, apparently just making idle conversation as he and Harwell rode along over the rolling hills and lush-grassed pastures.

"Yeah, Philadelphia, Boston, one o' them big cities. I don't recollect exactly which one. All I know is that there's more people there than I'd ever want to see in one place. Makes my skin crawl just thinkin' about bein' all crowded up like that."

"I don't reckon I blame you. What made him decide to come out here and buy a ranch?"

"I suppose he just wanted to be a cattleman. Lots of spreads are owned now by folks from back east, or over in England and such. The market's good, and a fella can make money at it if he's smart and lucky. Mr. Stockton's both of those things."

"How'd he make his money back east?"

Harwell shook his head. "Beats me. He don't never talk about it none. There's been a time or two, though, based on things that Miss Stockton said, I got the idea they didn't always have money. Reckon they might've been downright poor once."

"Miss Stockton seems like quite a lady."

"She is, and don't you ever forget it," Harwell said protectively. Clearly, Stockton wasn't the only one who looked out for Marie.

"Some of these other folks, though, I just don't know about them."

Harwell snorted. "Yeah, they're a prime bunch, ain't they? That Mr. Lawlor ain't bad, but he's a cold-eyed sort. I wouldn't want to play poker with him. But Ford and his wife . . ." Harwell shook his head. "Money, youth, and good looks are just plumb wasted on some people."

"What about that German fella?"

"The count's a windbag, but I reckon he's harmless enough. Same as Mr. and Miz Wilcox."

"And that blond girl, Miss Boothe?"

"She stays in her room most of the time, so I ain't seen that much of her. She's pretty enough, I'll give her that, but I ain't quite sure what the boss sees in her other than that. Seems dull as dishwater to me."

"So Mr. Stockton's sweet on her, is he?"

Harwell sniffed and drew himself up in his saddle. "I been talkin' too much. Appreciate it if you wouldn't go and tell Mr. Stockton I been flappin' my gums so."

Longarm grinned. "Hell, I ain't heard a word. We didn't talk about nothing but the ranch."

Harwell nodded and said, "I'm obliged."

They rode on, circling back toward the ranch headquarters, and Longarm risked one more question. "You know anything about this fella Thorne who has the boss worried?"

"Not a blessed thing," Harwell said. "He's not from around here. If he's one of Mr. Stockton's enemies, the grudge between 'em goes back to before he bought the Trident."

"When was that?"

"Just about a year ago."

Longarm eased himself in the saddle. "Well, like the boss said, a fella don't get to be a success in this world without making some enemies."

They talked about ranch matters the rest of the way, until just before they got back to the big house. Then Harwell reined in and motioned for Longarm to do the same. As they sat there on the ridge about a quarter of a mile from Trident headquarters, Harwell said seriously, "Were you tellin' the truth about bein' handy with a gun, Parker?"

"I've lived this long when there were some folks who didn't want me to," Longarm said.

Harwell nodded gravely. "I figured as much. You've got that look about you, like you've smelled a heap of gunsmoke. When the boss was talkin' about hirin' you as a regular ranch hand, I was willin' to put that feelin' aside. Plenty of fellas have been known to pull a gun when they had to, and that don't make them bad men. You wanted anywhere, Parker?"

"Nope. There's no paper out on me and never has been."

"All right. Reckon from here on out, whatever is between you and the boss is none of my business. I just wanted to make sure."

"Stockton is a lucky man to have a fella like you looking out for him, Ben."

"I ride for the brand," Harwell said stiffly. "Always have, always will."

Longarm just nodded. Between men such as him and Harwell, that was all that was needed. They were cut from the same cloth.

It was coming on toward evening. The ride around the Trident had taken most of the afternoon. As they unsaddled and cared for their horses, Longarm said, "I'll take this mount back to the livery stable when we go into Santa Fe to catch the train."

Harwell laughed. "Yeah, I reckon you won't need a horse in one o' them parlor cars."

The foreman went into the office attached to the bunkhouse while Longarm strolled toward the house. Lights glowed warmly in the windows. The rocking chairs on the gallery were empty, Longarm saw as he approached.

But one man was on the porch, and he stepped out of the shadows underneath the overhang as Longarm reached the steps. "Stop right there," a hard voice said, and from the sound of it, Longarm figured that a gun was backing up the words. The Gallic accent told him who the voice belonged to.

The time had finally come for the showdown between him and Pierre Dushane.

# Chapter 15

"Take it easy, old son," Longarm said calmly. "If all you want to do is palaver, well, I sort of had the same thing in mind."

"What is this . . . 'palaver'?" Dushane asked.

"Hash it over. Talk it all out, I reckon you'd say."

"*Certainement.* We need to talk, you and I, *M'sieur* Parker . . . or should I say, Marshal Long?"

Longarm stiffened. So Dushane *did* know who he was. But Dushane wasn't the only one who knew a secret.

"Say what you want," he told Dushane, "but I happen to know that your name ain't really Delacroix. Maybe we should both go spill what we know to Stockton."

Longarm heard the breath hiss between Dushane's teeth. "There is no need for that," the Frenchman said after a moment. "We will both be best served by discretion."

"Then put that gun away and walk with me," Longarm suggested.

"How do you know I have a gun?"

"I've heard that tone of voice before. Used it myself, in fact."

Dushane chuckled dryly. "Yes, I wager you have."

Longarm heard a rustle of cloth and figured Dushane was slipping a pistol back under his coat. The Frenchman came down the steps from the gallery. "Where shall we have this discussion?"

"Over by the corrals," Longarm decided. "There's nobody around them right now, and I don't reckon we want anybody eavesdropping on us."

"No," Dushane agreed, "we certainly do not."

They strolled toward the corrals. To the west, above the mountains, a faint rosy tinge remained in the sky, all that was left of the sunset. A few wispy clouds floated high above the peaks. Under other circumstances, Longarm would have thought it was a mighty pretty scene. Now, however, he was more concerned with what Dushane was going to say.

Longarm rested his arms on the top rail of the corral fence and hooked a boot on the bottom rail. Dushane stood next to him and said without preamble, "When I became aware that you were seeking *Mademoiselle* Boothe back in Kansas City, I made inquiries as to your identity. I was told that you were a federal marshal and that the man who accompanied you was a representative of the American State Department."

"Stewart Winchell was his name," Longarm said. "He was a pretty good fella."

"I had nothing to do with his death, if that is what concerns you. I believe that the ultimate responsibility lies at the feet of *M'sieur* Stockton."

Longarm nodded. "The same thought crossed my mind. I figure he paid Sparling, Horne, and Jackson to get rid of anybody who came looking for Miss Boothe. It was Horne you shot, there on the second floor of Red Mike's."

"I knew the man was either Horne or Jackson. I tracked them there through their association with the man Sparling. There was a ladder in the alley, so I thought I might be able to reach them before you did. Unfortunately, you were already doing battle with them when I arrived."

"You were dogging my trail the whole time I was in Kansas City, is that it?"

"Not entirely. I had already covered some of the same ground you did. But we arrived at the same destination, did we not?"

Longarm took out a cheroot, tipped the gasper into his mouth but didn't set fire to it. "Did you kill Horne to keep him from talking to me? What trail were *you* trying to cover?"

Dushane spread his hands and said, "You have made the error, *m'sieur*. Even though Horne fired at me and I would have been justified in killing him in defense of my own life, my intention was only to wound him, so that he could be questioned. I aimed for his shoulder. He leaped aside just as I pressed the trigger, however, and my shot struck him in the throat."

The story was believable enough, Longarm thought. He had had similar things happen to him. He might be willing to give Dushane the benefit of the doubt . . . but he wasn't going to admit that just yet.

"You were ahead of me in some ways," Longarm said, moving on to other matters. "You actually talked to Angela Boothe while she was in Kansas City. Someone saw you." He didn't mention Grace Dugan by name or identify her as the witness.

For a moment, Dushane didn't respond. Then he nodded and said, "This is true. I made *Mademoiselle* Boothe's acquaintance after observing her dining with *M'sieur* Stockton."

The light dawned in Longarm's brain. "It ain't really Angela you're interested in," he said. "It's Stockton. That's why you showed up here on the ranch claiming to be a friend of a friend of his."

"*Oui.* I was on the same train as you from Kansas City. I merely hired a buggy and driver to bring me out here last night, instead of waiting until this morning to arrive."

"Stockton didn't think that was a mite odd, you showing up in the middle of the night like that?"

"The name I used as a reference is a powerful one to him."

Longarm's teeth clenched on the cheroot. "Just who the hell are you, mister? What are you after?"

"That, unfortunately, I cannot say."

Anger welled up inside Longarm. "I've put my cards on the table with you, Dushane. You know I'm a lawman. Unless you're some sort of owlhoot, it won't hurt for you to come clean with me."

"Alas, my hands are tied. The best I can do, *M'sieur* Parker—and you notice, I have resumed using your alias, as that is in both of our best interests—is to assure you that we are both on the side of the angels in this matter. I am not the hooty owl."

"You're not mixed up in whatever crooked business Stockton is up to?"

"How do you know he is crooked, as you say?"

"He smuggled Angela Boothe out of Kansas City without anybody finding out about it. I know that because I checked at the train station and with all the stagecoach lines."

"*M'sieur* Stockton has a private railroad car," Dushane said. "*Mademoiselle* Boothe went aboard it in the darkness, with a hooded cloak over her head. That is what I suspect, at any rate."

"I figured as much," Longarm agreed. "Ted Sparling handled the baggage, and Stockton hired him and a couple of his tough pards to make sure nobody came looking for Angela. That led to a couple of killings. Like you said, Stockton's to blame for that, and that's enough to make him an outlaw in my book. But I don't know what else he's involved in. I got a feeling it ain't anything good, though."

"I would agree with that," Dushane murmured. "And to answer your question, *m'sieur,* my only connection with Stockton is a desire to find out the details of his nefarious plans."

Longarm thought it over for a moment and finally nodded. "It looks like we're on the same side, all right. I'd still like to know exactly who you are, mister, but I'm willing to let it ride for now. You keep quiet about me and I'll keep quiet about you."

"As you Americans say, we have a deal." Dushane paused, then added, "I fear, though, that I may have made this arrangement under somewhat false pretenses. It is possible Stockton already knows that you are a representative of the law."

"You reckon Sparling and the others might've got in touch with him before they tried to ambush me." Longarm's words were a statement, not a question.

"Telegraphic communication is quite swift. Those three miscreants might have wired Stockton and asked for advice on how to proceed."

"So he may have actually ordered them to kill me."

"Exactly."

Longarm had already worked that out for himself, but now he was even more sure of it. He wasn't clear on one thing, however.

"If Stockton knows I'm a lawman," he mused, "why did he hire me to go along on that trip to California with him and the rest of that crazy bunch? Why didn't he just try to have me killed again, or even do it himself?"

"Perhaps he wishes to discover the extent of the knowledge you have about him and his plans," Dushane suggested. "Or perhaps he does not wish to alarm or upset any of the others who are on the ranch at the moment, especially his sister. *Mademoiselle* Marie seems to have grown quite fond of you rather quickly."

"Yeah, I'd hate to think she's up to no good like her brother."

"And perhaps the explanation for *M'sieur* Stockton asking you to accompany them to California is quite simple." Dushane chuckled. "Perhaps he is just, as you Americans say, giving you enough rope to hang yourself, *M'sieur* Parker."

# Chapter 16

Longarm didn't get anything more out of Dushane. The Frenchman didn't tell him who he really was or why he was after Stockton, but Longarm was confident that both of them wanted to find out what Stockton planned to do with Angela Boothe. One possible answer immediately suggested itself. Angela was, after all, a beautiful young woman with a history of having a wicked streak.

But Stockton had to have something more in mind than a romp in the hay. Covering up an indiscretion like that wouldn't justify an attempt on the life of a federal lawman.

Longarm and Dushane walked back to the house after agreeing again to keep each other's secrets. They went in to find Stockton having a drink with Count von Steglitz, Edward Wilcox, Jason Lawlor, and Timothy Ford. None of the ladies were present.

"Dinner will be ready soon," Stockton said as he looked at Longarm and Dushane. "What were you two doing?"

Longarm grinned and said, "Just swapping yarns. Mr. Delacroix was telling me all about France. Sounds like quite a place."

*"Oui, M'sieur* Parker was curious about my home-land."

"Figure I'll never get there," Longarm put in. "Talking to a fella like Mr. Delacroix is as close as this old cow-hand will ever get."

Von Steglitz tossed back the liquor in his glass and said, "Why anyone would want to go to France is beyond me."

Dushane bristled at the count's arrogant, insulting tone. Longarm recalled that France and Germany had been at war with each other only a decade earlier, and both Du-shane and von Steglitz were old enough to have fought in the conflict. Clearly, both men harbored old grudges against the other's country.

Dushane, though, managed to control his anger and put a smile on his face. "I am willing to set aside politics while I visit this beautiful country," he said. "Perhaps, Count, you might do the same."

Von Steglitz shrugged and said, "Yah," though his agreement came with little grace.

Before any other words could be exchanged, the ladies swept into the room. Marie and Angela were beautiful, and even Claire Wilcox looked more attractive this eve-ning. The two younger women wore low-cut gowns that emphasized the supple curves of their figures.

Marie came straight to Longarm and linked her arm in his. "Did you enjoy your tour of the ranch this afternoon?" she asked.

"Sure did." Longarm looked at Stockton. "You've got a mighty nice spread here."

"Thank you," Stockton said. "We like it, don't we, Ma-rie?"

"It's home now," she murmured. "I would never want to move back east."

"Well, you won't have to." Stockton ushered them all into the dining room, where the Navajo servants had the table set beautifully and loaded down with mouth-watering food.

Without trying to be too obvious about it, Longarm kept an eye on Angela Boothe. The lovely blond Englishwoman hung on Grant Stockton's every word and pretty much ignored everyone else. Even when someone else spoke to her, she answered in distracted monosyllables. Longarm wasn't sure he had ever seen any gal quite so taken with a fella as Angela seemed to be with Stockton.

The food was excellent, and so was the wine with which it was washed down. When the meal was over, the men adjourned to the library that Marie had shown Longarm earlier in the day, while the women remained in the dining room. Stockton broke out brandy and cigars, and soon the air was thick with a blue haze of tobacco smoke.

Pierre Dushane went over to the shelves and brushed his fingertips over the cracked leather bindings of some of the old books. "You have quite an impressive collection, *M'sieur* Stockton," he said. "Some of these books must be priceless."

"You're familiar with them?" Stockton asked.

"Alas, no," Dushane replied with a shrug of his narrow shoulders. "I base my comment strictly on their obvious antiquity."

Stockton puffed on his cigar. "Just because a book is old doesn't make it valuable, at least not to me. It's what's inside it that counts."

"But of course."

Timothy Ford downed a healthy slug of brandy and said, "I've never been that much of a reader, myself."

"Somehow, that doesn't surprise me much," Jason Lawlor said with a thin, humorless smile.

Ford frowned as if trying to decide whether or not he ought to take offense at what Lawlor had just said, but then he reached for the brandy decanter and forgot about it.

Dushane was still interested in the books. "I have heard that some collectors will go to extraordinary lengths to obtain a particular volume they desire."

"Perhaps some of them do," Stockton said. He smiled. "I've always found that perseverance and money will get a man just about anything he wants, sooner or later."

Longarm stood to one side, smoking another of Stockton's cigars and taking an occasional sip of brandy. He didn't care much for the liquor. It was a mite too sweet for his taste.

He raised his glass with the others, though, when Stockton made a toast a few minutes later. "To California, gentlemen," the rancher said. "May our trip there be a pleasant and a profitable one."

"To California," Lawlor said, and Wilcox, Ford, and von Steglitz repeated the toast.

After drinking, Stockton turned to Dushane. "*M'sieur* Delacroix, is there any chance you might be able to accompany us? You said you were on a tour of the United States, and we'd be pleased to have you join us on this little jaunt to the West Coast."

"You mentioned profit," Dushane said. "I would not want to intrude on a business trip."

Stockton waved a hand casually. "Not at all. I meant profitable only in the sense that we plan to enjoy ourselves. Isn't that right, gentlemen?"

"Of course," Wilcox said, and Lawlor and Ford nodded. Wilcox went on, "You're more than welcome to join us, Delacroix. If Grant vouches for you, that's more than enough for me!"

"In that case . . ." Dushane lifted his glass again. "I join you in saying, 'To California!' "

Everyone drank again, except for Longarm, who had set his mostly full glass aside. "Reckon I'll take a look around outside before I turn in, boss," he said to Stockton.

"Wait just a minute, Parker." Stockton motioned him forward. "As the rest of you know, I've hired Parker here to work for me. What you may not be aware of is that he's going on the train with us, to sort of look out for us, I guess you'd say."

"A bodyguard?" von Steglitz said sharply. He drew himself up, his chest puffing out. "I cannot speak for the rest of you, but I have no need for a bodyguard."

"Take it easy, Otto," Stockton said, and there was a hard edge in his voice now. "I just want an experienced man along in case Thorne tries to cause any trouble for us."

Longarm tried to look at all of them at once, to see what sort of reaction Thorne's name provoked. Lawlor's jaw tightened angrily, and Wilcox looked worried, as did Timothy Ford. Von Steglitz muttered a curse in German. Clearly, the mysterious Lucius Thorne was more than just one of Stockton's business rivals. He seemed to be an enemy of the entire cartel, which was how Longarm was beginning to think of these five men.

Longarm remembered another cartel, the group of criminals that had plagued his old friend Jessie Starbuck for years, until it had been wiped out. He wondered if Stockton and his friends were just as sinister as that bunch had been. He hadn't seen any real evidence of that so far . . . but he hadn't seen anything that ruled it out, either.

"We don't have to worry too much about Thorne," Stockton told them. "I don't think he'll make a move against us. I'm just taking precautions."

"And that's a wise thing to do," Lawlor said with a nod. He looked at Longarm. "Better be on your toes, Parker."

"I figure on keeping my eyes open and my powder dry," Longarm said, and there was a lot of truth to that statement.

That was how he had stayed alive so far.

# Chapter 17

That night and the next day passed peacefully and uneventfully. Whoever Lucius Thorne was and whatever grudge he bore against Grant Stockton and the other men, he wasn't going to strike against the group while they were here on the Trident, with a full crew of tough cowboys close at hand. If there was going to be trouble, it was much more likely to take place on the train.

On several occasions Longarm tried to get close enough to Angela Boothe to strike up a conversation with her, but either she ignored him or Stockton deftly steered her away. Clearly, she was off-limits to everyone except Stockton, and that was the way she wanted it, too.

That wasn't the case with Marie Stockton, who was still quite friendly to Longarm and dropped hints that she could be even friendlier. For the time being, though, Longarm wasn't going to risk his position by dallying with the boss's sister, no matter how tempting the idea was. And it was mighty tempting.

When the time came, the whole bunch loaded up in buggies to head for Santa Fe. Ben Harwell had some of the hands load the group's baggage, which filled an entire wagon. These folks didn't travel lightly, Longarm thought as he looked at the pile of trunks and valises and carpetbags.

Harwell and a few cowboys rode along with them to bring back the buggies and the wagon to the ranch. Longarm took the point and led the way as the bunch pulled out from the Trident. Harwell rode alongside him.

"To tell you the truth," the foreman muttered so that only Longarm could hear him, "it's good riddance to most of these folks as far as I'm concerned. A passel of foreigners and Easterners got no place on a ranch."

"Can't say as I'd argue with you," Longarm replied. "The boss don't seem too bad, though."

"Oh, he's not. He pays good wages, and he's the best of the bunch, I reckon. Well, except for his sister. Miss Marie is mighty nice. You remember that while you're travelin' on that train with her, Parker."

Longarm grinned to himself. The old buzzard was a mother hen where Marie was concerned. He changed the subject by asking, "Has Stockton said how long he plans to stay out yonder in California?"

"Not to me, he ain't. Just told me to keep the ranch going while he was gone." Harwell snorted. "As if I'd ever let the place go to seed. I got more pride than that."

"Stockton's lucky to have you for a ramrod, old son."

"Been ridin' the range just about all my borned days. Wouldn't have no idea how to do nothin' else."

The group reached Santa Fe around noon and ate dinner in a local café before heading for the depot. The westbound was scheduled to arrive a little before two. According to the chalkboard by the door of the station, the train was expected to be on time.

It was, pulling in with a hiss of steam, a squeal of brakes, and a rattle of wheels on the iron rails. The cowboys from the Trident unloaded the baggage, with Harwell supervising as it was then loaded into the baggage car. Stockton's private car was parked on a siding along with a couple of other passenger cars that had been specially outfitted. The engineer backed up to them, and they were coupled on. The other members of Stockton's group would travel in those cars, in greater comfort than the usual passengers.

They all went aboard, gathering in Stockton's private car to drink a toast to the beginning of their journey. They were the toastingest bunch he had ever seen, Longarm thought. A short time later, with a puff of black smoke from the diamond stack on the locomotive, the train rolled out of Santa Fe, heading west, bound ultimately for Los Angeles.

Longarm walked from one end of the train to the other, looking for any signs of trouble. The passengers seemed to be the usual lot, mostly businessmen and families, a few soldiers, and a cowboy or three. The punchers would sleep sitting up on the hard benches. Their horses were probably back in one of the freight cars; that is, if they still had horses. They might be traveling with just their saddles.

Everybody seemed to be peaceful. Longarm didn't spot anybody he suspected of being one of Lucius Thorne's hired guns. It was hard to tell something like that for sure, though. Sometimes a deadly threat could be hidden behind a meek exterior.

That evening, the group dined in Stockton's private car. The railroad was going all out for the wealthy passengers and provided a fine meal. Longarm enjoyed it, and when he was finished, he stepped out onto the platform at the front of Stockton's car to have a smoke.

He had been there only a few minutes when the door behind him opened and Marie Stockton came out to join him. She had a lace shawl wrapped around her shoulders to guard against a chill from the night wind. She closed the door into the car and then stepped over to the iron railing, resting a hand on it.

"It's a beautiful night," she said to Longarm. "Look at those stars."

"Mighty pretty, all right," he agreed with a nod. "Of course, they ain't the only things around here that're pretty."

Marie laughed softly. "My, you are the gallant charmer, aren't you, Custis?"

"I try." Longarm grinned.

Without seeming to, she had moved closer to him so that he could smell the tantalizing fragrance of her hair. He almost thought he could feel the warmth coming from her body, but he knew that had to be his imagination.

It was the most natural thing in the world to slip an arm around her shoulders and draw her even closer. She came without hesitation, resting her head against him. She said, "I'm really glad that snake frightened my horse and I fell off. I might not have ever met you otherwise."

"I was already riding along the trail to the ranch," Longarm pointed out. "I reckon I'd have run into you either way."

"In other words, our meeting was fated to be."

Longarm chuckled. "I guess you could say that." He paused, then went on, "Sometimes fate ain't that kind, though. I'm just an old cowpuncher, nowhere near good enough to do any more than look at you in admiration, ma'am. And your brother would about have a stroke if he saw me holding you like this."

Marie snuggled even closer to him. "To hell with my brother," she said quietly but fervently. "He's always acted like he's in complete control of my life, and he doesn't have any right to be that way. I can make up my own mind what I want to do . . . and who I want to do it with."

With that, she lifted her face to his, and her lips were so close and so tempting that Longarm didn't have much choice except to bend down and kiss them.

Marie turned in his arms so that the whole length of her body was pressed tightly to his. She was soft and warm in his embrace, and her eager lips tasted sweet. Longarm rested one hand on the small of her back and brought the other up behind her head, slipping it into the thick mass of brown hair.

A part of his brain knew she was just rebelling against her brother's notion that he was in charge of her life. Longarm figured if he hadn't come along, sooner or later Marie would have found some other fella to throw herself at.

But he sensed an honesty in her as well, a genuine passion. And that passion had both of them a mite breathless when they finally broke the kiss long moments later.

"My goodness," Marie said when she had recovered her wits. "I . . . I suspected that I would enjoy kissing you, Custis, but I never thought it would be quite so . . . so stimulating."

The kiss had been stimulating as all hell, Longarm thought. His manhood had perked right up, the shaft lengthening and hardening until she had to be able to feel it poking against her belly. In fact, a mischievous smile suddenly played over her face, and she thrust her pelvis hard against him, making his arousal unmistakable.

"Is that for me?" she asked.

"I reckon you're the cause of it."

"Then it's up to me to do something about it, I suppose." She reached down, insinuating a slim hand between them so that she could caress him through his trousers. She felt along the shaft, exploring the size of it, and grew breathless again. "Oh, my goodness. I . . . I'm not sure all of it will fit. But I intend to find out."

"That ain't going to be easy," Longarm warned her. "This platform is about the most private place we'll be able to find on the train, and I don't reckon it'd be very comfortable."

Marie laughed. "No, I suppose not. But I happen to know there's an empty compartment in one of the Pullman cars up ahead." She sounded a little embarrassed as she added, "I bribed one of the porters to tell me about it."

"It's always a good thing to plan ahead, I reckon."

She lightly thumped a fist against his chest in a mock punch as she laughed again. Then she grew more serious as she went on, "Grant is talking business with his friends. He'll be so caught up in that for the next hour or so that he'll never notice I'm gone. Anyway, when he finishes talking, he'll have Angela waiting for him."

"She's staying in his car?"

"Yes." Marie frowned slightly in the moonlight. "Why should that matter to you, Custis?"

"I didn't say it did. I just like to know where everybody is, so I can keep track of 'em in case there's any trouble."

"That's right, your job is to look out for us, isn't it?" Marie seemed satisfied by his explanation. She came up on her toes and kissed him again, but only briefly this time. Still, the kiss packed a punch. "I'll slip up to that empty compartment first, and then you join me."

"How will I know which compartment you're in?" Longarm asked.

She pulled a lace handkerchief out of the bosom of her dress. "I'll hang this outside the curtains."

Longarm nodded. Marie slipped out of his arms and smiled at him as she went into the next car. He waited, giving her several minutes to get ready, and then went after her, striding through the special cars that had been hooked on in Santa Fe. They were empty at the moment, the other members of the group still being in Stockton's private car.

All the berths had been made up in the Pullmans. The aisle between the compartments was empty as Longarm stepped into it. He spotted the lace handkerchief peeking out from the curtains that closed off one of the berths and started toward it, the floor of the car swaying gently under his booted feet as the train rocked along the rails. He had made love on trains before and always enjoyed it. He hoped Marie would, too.

As he reached the compartment where she was waiting for him, he paused and leaned toward the curtains. He wanted to be sure he had the right one. It would be mighty embarrassing if he crawled into the berth only to find that he was sharing it with some middle-aged matron from Topeka.

"Marie?" he whispered.

A curtain suddenly rustled behind him, and he heard the slap of shoe leather on the floor. Longarm started to turn, just in time for the gun butt sweeping down at him to smash into the side of his head.

# Chapter 18

The blow hurt like hell, but it was only a glancing one and failed to do anything more than stun Longarm for a second. He caught hold of the curtain to keep himself from falling and struck out instinctively with his other hand, slamming a fist into the chest of the man who had pistol-whipped him. The man staggered back across the aisle toward the berth from which he had emerged.

Longarm got a look at the man then. He was tall, skinny, had an ax blade of a nose and a drooping black mustache. He wore a derby and a somewhat shabby tweed suit. As he caught his balance, he flipped the gun around in his hand and tried to bring the weapon to bear on Longarm.

The big lawman had recovered his wits by now, though, and he lunged across the aisle to grab the gunman's wrist. Longarm knew he couldn't draw his own Colt and start throwing lead in the cramped confines of this Pullman car where heavy curtains were all that closed off the compartments. It would be all too easy for a wild slug to hit an innocent person, maybe even Marie Stockton.

Longarm locked his fingers around the gunman's wrist

and put all the strength of his rangy body into a savage twist. The man cried out in pain as bones grated together inside his arm. The pistol slipped out of his fingers and thumped to the floor of the car.

That wasn't his only weapon, though. He brought his knee up sharply, causing Longarm to turn aside so that he took the blow on his thigh rather than in his privates. That gave his attacker the chance to reach under his coat with his left hand and pull out a knife.

Longarm let go of the man's wrist and jerked back to avoid a vicious slash of the knife. Light from the lamp that lit the corridor glittered on the blade as it whipped past his face, only inches away. The missed stroke threw the man off balance. Longarm hooked a toe behind his leg and pulled, yanking the man off his feet. The man grabbed Longarm's sleeve as he fell, however, and hauled the federal man down on top of him.

Longarm had to writhe like a snake for a second to keep the man from gutting him with the knife. He finally got his fingers on the wrist of that hand and forced it to the side. With his other hand Longarm threw a short, hard punch that smacked into the man's jaw and caused the back of his head to bounce on the floor. By now, Longarm was vaguely aware of shouted curses and questions as the commotion drew the attention of the passengers in the compartments. Some of those passengers had opened the curtains and looked out to see the two men locked in their deadly struggle.

A gun roared from the front end of the car. The bullet sang past Longarm's ear with a wicked whine and smacked into the door at the rear end. Longarm jerked his head up and saw another man wearing a suit and a derby standing just inside the car, smoke curling from the barrel of the gun in his hand. The first man clearly had a confederate who also wanted Longarm dead and wasn't worried about hitting one of the passengers.

The first attacker was still stunned from the punch Longarm had landed. The big lawman flung himself off that man, landing belly down on the floor as the second gunman fired again. Now the air inside the car was filled with frightened but muffled screams as the passengers ducked back into their berths and tried to get as far away from the aisle and as far out of the line of fire as they could.

Longarm rolled onto his side so that he could get at his Colt. The revolver seemed to leap from its holster into his hand. It bucked against Longarm's palm as he triggered a shot. The bullet caught the second gunman in the chest and drove him back against the half-open door behind him. He grunted in pain and tried to get off another shot, but the gun in his hand seemed too heavy for him to hold it up. The barrel dropped toward the floor, and when the man's finger finally managed to squeeze the trigger as the result of a dying nerve impulse, the bullet went into the planks at his feet. A trickle of blood ran from the man's mouth as he pitched forward onto his face.

The sound of someone clambering awkwardly to his feet made Longarm swing his head around. He saw the first man diving toward the rear door of the car, obviously giving up on the assassination attempt. Longarm twisted around and tried to draw a bead on him, but the rear door slammed and the man was gone. Longarm scrambled up and went after him.

A part of him wanted to stay and make sure Marie was all right, but he also wanted to catch the surviving bushwhacker and make him talk. He remembered now seeing the two men sitting together in one of the coaches earlier in the day, but they had seemed harmless enough and he had taken them for traveling salesmen. That just went to show that he'd been right about not always being able to tell by looking whether someone was dangerous. Longarm knew the two men didn't have any personal grudge against him—he had never seen them before today—so the question was who had hired them to kill him.

The mysterious Lucius Thorne . . . or Grant Stockton?

That last idea didn't make much sense, Longarm thought fleetingly as he rushed out of the car after the gunman. If Stockton still wanted him dead, there had been plenty of opportunities to arrange that while Longarm was on the Trident Ranch. On the other hand, he realized, maybe Stockton didn't want to have somebody murdered right there on his own land.

Maybe the gunman could give Longarm some answers.

Unfortunately, he seemed to have vanished.

There was no sign of the man on the platform between cars. The next one back was the first of the special cars. Longarm jerked the door open and looked inside. This was a Pullman car, too, but with larger, more luxurious compartments and a small sitting room. Edward Wilcox was just entering the car from the other end. He stopped short, eyes widening as he saw Longarm standing there with a gun in his hand.

"You see anybody come in here?" Longarm asked sharply.

"No, but I just got here," Wilcox replied. "What's wrong, Parker?"

Longarm bit back a curse and used the barrel of the Colt to rip aside the curtains over the berths on both sides of the car. They were empty. The gunman hadn't come this way.

That left only one way for him to have escaped—up.

Longarm holstered the revolver and grabbed the rungs of the ladder that led to the roof of the Pullman car where Marie supposedly had been waiting for him. As he climbed, an awful thought crossed his mind. What if *Marie* had set up the ambush? She was the one who had asked him to come to that Pullman car and told him to look for that lace handkerchief, and the gunman had been waiting right across the aisle to jump him.

Grim-faced, Longarm shoved that possibility out of his mind for now. He could investigate it later, once he had his hands on that skinny, derby-hatted son of a bitch.

He paused before poking his head up when he reached the top of the ladder. He didn't want to make himself too easy of a target. Sure enough, when he risked a quick look, a gun blasted at the far end of the car and the bullet ricocheted off into the night, kicking up splinters from the roof as it did so. Longarm ducked, then looked again and saw the gunman leaping from that car to the next one. It was a daring move, jumping from car to car on a swaying train, but clearly he was a desperate man.

Longarm pulled himself onto the roof and came up in a crouch. His jaw was clenched tight. He had found himself in this situation before in his career as a lawman, chasing a man who wanted to kill him on top of a moving train. It was hell on the nerves. But he had no choice except to go ahead.

The man twisted around, saw Longarm coming after him, and snapped off another shot. Longarm crouched lower as Colt flame bloomed in the darkness. This bullet didn't come close enough for him to hear it, though. Accurate shooting was almost impossible under these conditions. That was one reason he left his Colt in its holster. Another was that he wanted to capture the gunman, not kill him. In the exchange of shots down below, he hadn't had any choice. He had been forced to shoot to kill then, because of the possibility that the second gunman might hurt someone else.

The man he was after now hurried on toward the front of the train. Longarm ran after him, timing his jump and then leaping the gap between cars just as the gunman had. He wondered if the hombre intended to try to reach the locomotive.

The answer to that was no, Longarm saw as his quarry started climbing down the ladder at the far end of the next car. Longarm grabbed the ladder at the end where he was and swung down recklessly, his legs hanging out over empty air for a second before they arched in and his feet landed on the platform. He yanked his gun out and threw the door open.

This was a coach car filled with wooden benches, cheaper seats where folks had to sleep sitting up, if they slept at all. It was full of families, and there were quite a few startled shouts as Longarm charged past them toward the front of the car. "Get down!" he called to them in case more shooting broke out. "Down!"

The front door of the car flew open. The gunman lunged inside, but he didn't go far. His left arm shot out and looped around the throat of a startled boy about twelve years old. As the boy's mother screamed, the gunman jerked the youngster in front of him to use as a shield. The gun in his hand roared deafeningly as he fired at Longarm.

Longarm felt as much as heard the wind-rip of the bullet past his head. He couldn't risk a shot, and now the car was plunged into chaos as women screamed, men cursed, children cried, and everybody tried to scramble out of the way of the flying lead. Longarm dropped to a knee and lifted the Colt, but he didn't have a clear shot. The boy was in the way.

Had to give the youngster credit for quick thinking in a crisis. He reached in his pocket, pulled out a Barlow knife, yanked it open with his teeth, and brought the knife back to plunge the blade into the gunman's thigh. The man yelled in pain and loosened his grip enough for the boy to twist away from him. As the boy dived out of the line of fire, Longarm aimed for a split second and then squeezed the trigger.

The shot went where he wanted it to, smack-dab

113

through the right shoulder of the gunman. He dropped his revolver as the impact of the slug sent him flying backward through the open door. He sprawled on the platform between cars.

Longarm leaped up and ran toward the front end of the car. He had just wounded the gunman. The bastard would live to answer some questions, the most important of which would be who had hired him and his partner to bushwhack Longarm.

But as Longarm closed in, he saw the wounded man trying to struggle to his feet. He wasn't going to give up, despite having a bullet-smashed shoulder. He came to his feet, reeled, lost his balance. . . .

And plunged right into the gap between cars.

Longarm stopped short, horror etched on his face as he heard the man's scream and the way it was abruptly cut off. "Somebody pull the emergency cord!" he snapped at the passengers, but even as he said it, he knew the gesture was too late. The gunman hadn't had a chance. He wasn't going to be answering any questions, either, not after the wheels of the train had probably cut him plumb in two.

The train screeched and jolted and lurched to an abrupt halt as one of the passengers did as Longarm had said and yanked the emergency cord. Longarm grabbed the back of one of the benches to brace himself while the train shuddered and finally stopped.

Then he turned and headed for the rear of the train, ignoring the frightened and angry questions of the passengers he passed. He still had to find out what had happened to Marie Stockton.

# Chapter 19

To his relief, Longarm saw that Marie seemed to be all right. She was standing in the aisle of the Pullman car where the ambush attempt had taken place, along with a dozen or more of the other passengers and the harried-looking conductor. The conductor was trying to calm the fears of the frightened mob. When Marie spotted Longarm coming toward them, she called out, "Custis! Are you all right?"

She rushed into his arms as he walked up. She wore a silk dressing gown belted tightly around her waist. The fabric clung to her body, revealing its supple curves. Longarm enjoyed the feel of her as she hugged him, but he hadn't forgotten his earlier suspicions. He could delay confronting her about them, however. He didn't want to get into that with the conductor and the other passengers standing right there.

"I'm fine," he assured Marie. "How about you? You're not hurt?"

She looked up at him, frowning in puzzlement. "Why would I be hurt? It looked like you were the one those men were after."

"A few slugs went flying around," Longarm said. "I was afraid you might have been hit."

The conductor said, "The only one who was hit was that fella down there." He motioned toward the body of the man Longarm had been forced to ventilate. "He's dead. You better do some talking, mister. I want to know why this fracas broke out on my train."

Under other circumstances, Longarm could have pulled out his badge and bona fides and smoothed over the conductor's ruffled feelings. As it was, though, he didn't want to announce his identity as a lawman, even though it appeared that someone—likely Grant Stockton and maybe others—was already aware of it. Instead, he let some genuine anger seep into his voice as he said, "I'd like to know why, too. That fella and another gent jumped me and tried to kill me. All I did was protect myself."

"There were two of them? Where's the other one?"

Grim-faced, Longarm replied, "He fell between two of the cars up ahead. I don't reckon there's much left of him . . . not in one piece, anyway."

Marie shuddered, and so did several of the other women standing around in the aisle. A man muttered a low-voiced oath that sounded as much like a prayer as a curse. The conductor asked, "Is that why you pulled the emergency cord?"

Longarm nodded, not bothering to explain that he hadn't pulled the cord personally. The end result was the same. He said, "I reckon we better get a lantern and take a *paseo* back along the tracks."

"I guess so," the conductor agreed reluctantly.

A new voice spoke up from the rear door, rapping out peremptory questions. "What's going on here? Why have we stopped?"

Marie took a sharply indrawn breath and paled slightly as Longarm glanced at her. She moved a step backward and edged behind the partially drawn curtain in front of the compartment. From there she couldn't be seen as her brother strode into the car, his face dark with anger and concern.

Eager to stay on the wealthy rancher's good side, the conductor said quickly, "There's been a little trouble, Mr. Stockton, but nothing you need to be worried about—"

"The hell you say," Stockton interrupted. "Parker there works for me. What happened, Parker?"

"A couple of men jumped me, tried to kill me." Longarm gestured at the corpse Stockton had stepped over on his way into the car. "There's one of 'em. Ever seen him before?"

Stockton glanced down at the man and then shook his head. "No, but I'd wager that he works for Lucius Thorne. That man will stop at nothing to get his way."

"We're going to have to have us a talk about Thorne," Longarm said, a hard edge in his voice. "I can't do my job if I'm in the dark about what's going on."

Stockton jerked his head in a nod. "I think you're right, Parker. Come on back to my car when you're through here."

"All right."

Stockton said to the conductor, "How long will we be stopped?"

"Not long, I hope," the man replied.

Stockton nodded again and left. The other passengers were drifting back to their berths. Longarm glanced over at the compartment where Marie was hidden. She pulled the curtain back slightly and peeked out at him. "Is Grant gone?" she whispered.

Longarm nodded. "Stay there. I want to talk to you."

From the sly look on the conductor's face, the man had recognized Marie as Stockton's sister, and he had to know from her behavior that something illicit was going on. But anybody who worked for the railroad knew that such things took place on trains all the time, so Longarm hoped

117

the man also knew how to keep his mouth shut.

He tried to ensure that as he and the conductor walked along the tracks a few minutes later. A lantern swung from the conductor's hand. Longarm said, "I reckon it'd be a good idea not to mention that you saw Miss Stockton in that Pullman car tonight."

"I have to look out for the welfare of my passengers," the man said. "Especially important passengers like Mr. Stockton. I'm sure he'd be grateful to know that his sister was all right, even though she was in that car when the shooting took place."

Longarm grunted. "Grateful, huh?" He knew good and well what the conductor meant, and when it came to bribes, Longarm couldn't hope to compete with Grant Stockton. He had to play the card he had wanted to keep in the hole. "Well, the federal government would be just as grateful if you'd keep things to yourself, old son."

The conductor stopped short and swung around so that the glow from the lantern played over Longarm's rugged face. "The federal government?" he repeated.

"That's right. The State Department, the Justice Department, and the chief marshal's office in Denver. Hell, Lemonade Lucy herself might feel kindly toward you," he added, using the nickname of the First Lady, the wife of President Rutherford B. Hayes.

"You're a lawman," the conductor said, stating the obvious.

"That's right."

"Does Mr. Stockton know that?"

"What Stockton knows or don't know ain't none of your business, friend. Now, are we clear on that?"

"Yeah," the conductor said grudgingly. "I guess so. I won't say anything."

Longarm wasn't sure the man was completely sincere, but right now that pledge was the best he could do. He

118

said, "Let's go on and take a look at that hombre who fell."

It was every bit as grisly a sight as Longarm had expected to find. The wheels of the train had chopped the skinny gunman into pieces, making him skinnier than ever. The conductor, hardened though he was by the sight of previous accidents, walked away from the railroad embankment and threw up. When he came back, shaky and white-faced, Longarm took the lantern and held it so that the light shone on the face of the dead man.

"Know who he is?"

The conductor shook his head. "No. I remember seeing him and his partner when they got on the train at Santa Fe, but I don't think I ever saw them before that." He wiped the back of his hand across his mouth. "I'll get some porters and a piece of canvas. We'll gather up the . . . pieces . . . and put them in the baggage car, I guess."

Longarm left him to that gruesome task and walked back to the train. He had that conversation with Stockton to get to, but he wanted to talk to Marie first.

He swung up into the Pullman car and saw that the body there had been removed. The aisle was empty again, as all the passengers had retreated into their compartments. Longarm went to the one where Marie had been waiting for him earlier. The telltale handkerchief was gone now, but Longarm knew which compartment it was without that. He leaned close to the curtains and said quietly, "Marie?"

"Come in, Custis," she said.

Longarm pushed the curtain aside and stepped into the shallow compartment with its pull-down bed. He let the curtain fall closed behind him. A small oil lamp lit the compartment and showed him Marie Stockton lying in the berth, the covers pulled up to her chin. She smiled at Longarm and sat up, so that the covers fell away from her. From the first sight of her bare shoulders, Longarm figured she was nude under there, and he was right. His eyes were drawn to her firm, bare breasts, creamy globes the size of apples tipped with small pink nipples. She was mighty tempting, no doubt about that.

"Thank God you're here at last, Custis," Marie said, her voice a husky, sensuous whisper. "Come. Make love to me."

It cost him an effort, but Longarm said in a hard voice, "Nope. Not just yet."

# Chapter 20

She stared at him in disbelief shaded with anger. "What? What do you mean, not yet? I've been waiting for you—"

"We got to talk first," Longarm said. He took off his hat, which he had retrieved from the floor of the aisle where it had fallen off during the struggle with the bushwhacker, and sat down at the foot of the berth.

Suddenly shy, Marie pulled up the sheet and covered her breasts. "What's wrong, Custis?" she asked. "I know you might be a little upset, considering everything that happened—"

Again he interrupted her. "Having a couple of hombres try to kill him does tend to put a fella off his feed."

"But you're all right. You said so."

"I ain't hurt except for a little bump on the noggin, but I'm mighty curious. I want to know who those fellas were and why they tried to bushwhack me."

"I don't blame you, but I don't see how you can find out anything tonight."

With a slight lurch, the train started moving again. Longarm knew that meant the conductor and the porters had retrieved the mangled corpse from along the tracks.

"I can ask you if you know anything about it," Longarm said.

Marie stared at him uncomprehendingly for a moment, but then her gaze grew even angrier as she figured out what he meant. "You think *I* had something to do with those men attacking you?"

"You're the one who suggested we meet up here," he pointed out. "And one of them was waiting right across the aisle from the compartment you marked with that handkerchief."

"Get out," she said coldly. "If you believe that I could have anything to do with those men trying to hurt you, then just leave."

"I ain't said that I believe it. I'm just asking, that's all."

"Yes, but how can I prove to you that I didn't?" she shot back. "You either trust me or you don't, Custis, and since you obviously don't . . ."

"Your brother thinks they worked for Lucius Thorne."

Marie sniffed. "That seems like a much more plausible explanation to me, too, but then, I'm not as suspicious as you are."

This was going badly, Longarm thought. He didn't hardly see how it could have gone any other way. Confronting Marie was bound to ruin the plans she had for the evening. Yet he'd had to know.

"What can you tell me about Thorne?"

"How would I know anything about him? He's just some business rival of Grant's. I've never met the man, never even seen him."

"Did you get a look at the two men who jumped me?"

She shook her head. "Not really. Just a glimpse while all the fighting was going on. But I don't remember ever seeing either of them before, if that's what you're getting at."

Longarm thought she was telling the truth. Her hurt

feelings could have been an act, but he didn't think so.

It was possible the bushwhackers could have been looking for an opportunity to kill him. They might have even seen him kissing Marie on the platform between cars, though they would have had to be spying on him from one of the special cars in order to do so. Still, that wasn't beyond the realm of possibility. If that was what had happened, they could have seen Marie slip into the Pullman compartment and guessed that she was waiting there for a rendezvous with Longarm. The theory might or might not be correct, but at least it held together reasonably well and vindicated Marie.

Of course, it was still possible that Stockton had sent the men after him, Longarm thought. He couldn't rule that out, either. The whole case was still too murky to draw any solid conclusions.

"I reckon I owe you an apology," he said to Marie.

"I don't know if I accept it. What makes you believe me now when you suspected me earlier?"

"I reckon I just had to hear it from you, personal-like."

She glared at him for a long moment, but eventually a faint smile tugged at her lips. "I guess when you're paid to be a bodyguard, you have to be suspicious," she said. The sheet slipped a little as she leaned forward, revealing more of her shoulders and the top of the cleft between her breasts. "But you don't have to be suspicious of *me,* Custis. I'd never do anything to hurt you."

"Well, that's mighty good to know," he said. He reached up and cupped her chin. When she didn't pull away, he leaned closer and pressed his lips to hers. She let go of the sheet entirely, allowing it to fall to her waist again, and wrapped her arms around his neck.

Her warm breasts flattened against his chest as she pressed herself closer to him. After a moment, Longarm broke the kiss and moved his lips down to her throat. He slid them over her smooth skin, trailing kisses until he reached her left breast. He cupped the firm mound of female flesh and drew the erect nipple into his mouth, sucking gently on it. Marie said, "Ahhh . . ." and stroked his hair. He moved to her other breast and sucked and licked that nipple as well. She lay back as his kisses traveled farther south. Throwing the sheet back, she opened her legs and spread her thighs wide. The feminine cleft at the apex of the triangle of dark brown hair was pink and moist and inviting.

Longarm accepted the invitation and plunged his tongue into it.

Her hips bucked up off the berth and her thighs squeezed against his ears as he penetrated her with his oral caress. His thumbs spread the fleshy folds even wider. His tongue explored the length of her crevice and toyed with the little nubbin of flesh that crowned it. Marie cried out softly in the throes of the passion he aroused in her. As Longarm continued licking and sucking and stroking with his tongue, he slipped a hand underneath her buttocks and used a finger to tease the puckered brown opening between them. It seemed to suck his finger in.

Marie began to shudder. She bit her lip to keep from crying out as a climax rippled through her. The delta of her sex was flooded with her heated juices. Longarm kept lapping as a second culmination rocked Marie.

Breathlessly, she said, "Now . . . now you, Custis!" She took hold of his shoulders and tugged him into the berth beside her.

Longarm slipped his gunbelt off and laid it on the floor beside the bunk. Then he let Marie do the rest of the work of stripping off his duds. When she pulled down his long underwear and allowed his shaft to spring free, it stood up tall and straight and thick. Marie wrapped both hands around the pole, leaned over it, and began to lick avidly around the crown.

Longarm closed his eyes and gave himself over to the

pleasure of what she was doing to him. She was good at it, licking his shaft from base to tip, using her tongue to tease the opening at the end, cupping his heavy sacs in her hand and rolling them back and forth gently. Finally she opened her mouth wide and took him in, closing her warm lips around the throbbing organ. Longarm opened his eyes then to enjoy the delicious sight of his manhood being engulfed by her mouth.

No man could withstand such exquisite torment for very long. Exceptional though he was in some areas, Longarm was still human, so after a few minutes of the French lesson, he said huskily, "Unless you want everything I got to give mighty quick, darlin', you'd better ease up."

In response to his warning, she swallowed even more of his shaft and began sucking harder. Longarm threw caution to the winds. If that was what she wanted, he was more than willing to oblige. When he felt his climax boiling up, he didn't try to suppress it. Instead he rode along eagerly on the wave of passion that carried him to the crest.

His climax burst from him in spurt after white-hot spurt of thick, scalding seed. Marie sucked and swallowed, working hard to keep up with the torrent. She couldn't quite manage to do so. Some of his juices overflowed her mouth and dribbled down her chin. When she finally had to gasp and lift her mouth from his shaft, he was still emptying himself. Strands of the stuff landed on her cheeks and nose and chin. She caught her breath and plunged down on him again, wrapping her fingers around the massive pole and squeezing so she could milk the last few precious drops from it.

At last she collapsed with her face nestled in the thick mat of hair that covered his groin. Longarm was breathing so hard he felt like he had just run a mile in the desert. He reached down and stroked her hair where it was spread out over his belly. He could feel Marie's breasts moving against his thighs as her chest heaved from her own efforts.

When she finally lifted her head and smiled up at him, Longarm took a corner of the sheet and used it to wipe the stickiness from her face. She said, "I . . . I never knew a woman could experience so much pleasure just from . . . what I did to you. Thank you, Custis."

"Reckon I'm the one who ought to be thanking you." He took hold of her shoulders and urged her to slide up over him until her nude body was sprawled full-length on his. When she kissed him the taste of each other's juices blended muskily. Longarm slid his hands down her back to the swell of her buttocks, cupped and parted them. Marie thrust her pelvis against him.

"What else are we going to do?" she asked in a whisper.

"Everything under the sun," Longarm told her, "but not right now, I'm sorry to say."

She raised herself slightly and frowned down at him. "Well, I didn't mean right away, since you just . . . but in a little while . . ."

"I hope so," Longarm said, and meant it. "But right now I got to go talk to your brother."

Her frown deepened. "You're leaving?"

"It ain't like I want to," he assured her. "But your brother's waiting for me. We got to have a talk about this fella Thorne. It's time he put his cards on the table."

"Maybe. I guess I understand. You want to know what you're up against, and I don't blame you for that." She pouted prettily. "But I'd rather you stay up against me for the rest of the night."

"Me, too," Longarm said. He was relieved to see that she was disappointed but not furious with him. "If you want to stay here, I'll be back as soon as I can."

"I'll be waiting," Marie promised.

And then she gave him one more hot, searching kiss. Longarm figured that was her way of telling him not to waste any time . . . not that he intended to.

# Chapter 21

The Pullman car had one of those newfangled water closets at the back of it, so Longarm stopped there and washed up a mite, so he wouldn't smell like he had just come from a whorehouse when he sat down to talk with Grant Stockton. When he walked back through the two special cars, he heard snoring coming from several of the berths, along with the sounds of lovemaking from one of them. He figured that was where Timothy and Millicent Ford were staying, but you never could tell about things like that. Despite their staid exteriors, the Wilcoxes might just get frisky from time to time.

Pierre Dushane was in the sitting room of the second car, smoking a cigar as he read a newspaper. He looked up at Longarm and said, "Good evening, *M'sieur* Parker."

"Mister Delacroix," Longarm drawled in return.

"I hear there was a bit of excitement earlier. Someone tried to do you harm?"

"You could say that."

"It would be wise to remain alert during the rest of this journey."

Longarm went to the rear door and looked back over

his shoulder at the Frenchman, saying, "That's just what I intend to do, old son."

He knocked on the door of Stockton's private car and opened it when Stockton called, "Yes, what is it?" The wealthy cattleman was pacing back and forth restlessly over the expensive rug on the floor of the car. He stopped when he saw who his visitor was. "Parker! You sure as hell took your time about getting back here."

"I got delayed a mite," Longarm said, not adding that most of the time had been taken up by having his cock sucked by Stockton's sister. The fella didn't need to hear that.

Stockton gestured impatiently toward a pair of armchairs. "Sit down," he said. "You want a cigar, or something to drink?"

"Not now," Longarm said with a shake of his head. "What I really want is for us to clear the air about this hombre Thorne. I know you and him are enemies, and you don't think he'd stop at anything to get what he wants, including murder."

Stockton sank into the other chair. "I *know* Thorne wouldn't stop at murder. I suspect he killed an agent of mine in Paris. Not personally, of course—Thorne isn't the sort of man to dirty his own hands—but he had it done, I'm sure of that."

"He killed a man over business?"

A cold smile touched Stockton's face. "What better reasons to kill than wealth and power?" Without waiting for an answer, he went on, "But no, not in this case. Thorne had my agent murdered so he wouldn't get his hands on something that both Thorne and I want."

"And what would that be?"

Stockton shook his head. "I'm afraid I can't tell you that, Parker."

Longarm started to get to his feet, not bothering to hide

his anger. "Damn it, I thought we were going to lay our cards on the table—"

"Wait!" Stockton motioned for Longarm to sit down again. "I'm sorry, Parker—and that's not something that a man like me says often or easily."

As Longarm sank back down in the chair, Stockton leaned forward and clasped his hands together. "There are some things that have to remain secret for the time being, but I assure you of this: eventually, you'll know the truth, all of it, and if you do your job, you'll share in a great reward, Parker . . . greater, perhaps, than you can even imagine. For now, though, let me just say that I have something Lucius Thorne wants very much, so much that he would kill for it. He would kill me and anyone else standing in his way."

"I thought you said Thorne got whatever it was the two of you were after in Paris."

"Well, I didn't say as much," Stockton responded with a shrug, "but that happens to be true. Thorne won that round of our battle . . . but I'm going to win the war. Because you see, Parker, the thing that Thorne stole from me is worthless without something else." Stockton lounged back in his chair and smirked. "And I've got that something else."

Longarm hazarded a guess. "You're on your way to California to meet Thorne, aren't you?"

"That's right. We've struck a bargain of sorts. But that won't stop him from trying to double-cross me. He would gladly kill me and all my associates and take what he wants. That way he wouldn't have to deal with me when the time comes." Stockton laughed. "I assure you, Parker, I intend to drive a hard bargain. Thorne won't get everything he wants, and the price for what he does get will be high."

Longarm was getting tired of all this beating around the bush. Stockton wasn't going to reveal much of anything else. But the conversation hadn't been a total waste of time. Longarm had a pretty good idea now that the two men who had attacked him tonight had been working for Lucius Thorne. Stockton might have wanted him dead while he was poking around back in Kansas City, but now it seemed that Stockton had a use for him and would want to keep him alive, even knowing that Longarm was a federal lawman. This was a deep game they were playing, with everybody pretending not to know things that they really knew.

Longarm indulged a last bit of curiosity. "These folks who are traveling with you," he asked, "what's their part in all this?"

"They really are business associates of mine. Well, except for Delacroix, of course. I probably shouldn't have asked him to come along, simply for the sake of his own safety, but I indulged a whim. You could say I was just trying to be a good host."

Dushane could take care of himself, Longarm knew, but Stockton might not be aware of that. Stockton had no way of knowing about Dushane's part in the fracas back in Kansas City.

"I reckon Thorne had his men bushwhack me tonight so that I'd be out of the way whenever he tries to grab whatever it is you've got."

Stockton nodded. "That's the way I see it. Now you know how serious—and how dangerous—this situation really is. Still want to come along for the ride, Parker?"

"More than ever," Longarm said, and he meant every word of it. He still didn't trust Stockton and still wanted to get to the bottom of whatever dirty business the man was up to.

But after those hired guns of Thorne's had tried to kill him, Longarm had a personal reason for sticking with this case, too. When the cleanup came, it was going to be a hell-roarer.

• • •

True to her promise, Marie was waiting for Longarm in
the Pullman compartment when he got back. They spent
a very pleasant couple of hours doing all sorts of things
with and to each other and finally went to sleep in each
other's arms. Before they dozed off, Longarm asked her,
"Won't your brother wonder where you are?"

"I made up the berth in my compartment to look like
there's someone sleeping in it," she answered sleepily.
"Even if Grant checks on me, which I don't think he'll
do, he'll just think I'm asleep and won't bother me."

Longarm accepted that explanation. Marie knew her
brother better than he did.

He woke up before dawn the next morning with her
straddling him, hips pumping as she rode his erect organ.
Both of them climaxed quickly, with Longarm holding
Marie's hips and thrusting up into her as he spurted. As
soon as she caught her breath, she kissed him lightly on
the lips, pulled her clothes on, and slipped out of the compartment to go back where she was supposed to be.

The entire group ate breakfast together in Stockton's
private car. Longarm noticed that Stockton took special
care to see that Angela Boothe received a particular cup
of coffee. It probably had a dollop of that brandy she liked
so much in it.

He wondered just what sort of drug Stockton was using
to keep Angela in a half-stupor. He had seen people who
were doped up before, and it hadn't taken him long to
tumble to what was going on. He had a pretty good idea,
too, that Angela was the something Stockton had that Lucius Thorne wanted. Plenty of men throughout history had
fought over a pretty girl, Longarm mused, all the way
back to Troy and that gal Helen, but this was different.
Angela Boothe hadn't launched a thousand ships with her
beauty or toppled any timeless towers, but there sure had
been some powder burned over her. Why?

That was what Longarm intended to learn when the train reached Los Angeles, if not before.

During the night, the train had crossed into Arizona Territory just beyond Gallup, New Mexico, south of Shiprock and the Four Corners country. Longarm had ridden all over those parts and had a lot of memories, both good and bad, of them. The locomotive rolled on toward Flagstaff, past the Petrified Forest and the Painted Desert, coming into sight of snow-capped peaks and pine-covered foothills. To the north was the huge canyon of the Colorado River. Longarm liked Arizona. It was big country, rugged country, good country.

The train was still about ten miles east of Flagstaff when with a shrill, frantic whistle from the engine, brakes screamed, couplings clashed, and unsuspecting passengers were thrown off their feet as the whole shebang came to a sliding, screeching halt. Like a lot of other people, Longarm found himself on the floor.

He wasn't a bit surprised a moment later when guns began to roar outside the train.

# Chapter 22

Longarm had been walking through the sitting room of one of the special cars when the train came to its abrupt, bone-jarring halt. Now he scrambled to his feet and lunged over to one of the windows, drawing his Colt as he peered out to see what was going on.

Timothy and Millicent Ford were in the sitting room, too, and had been tossed off a divan to land in the floor. Timothy was on the bottom and seemed stunned. His wife had fallen on top of him. She was able to get up. She grabbed Longarm's arm and screamed, "Oh, my God! Oh, my God! What is it? Are we being attacked by Indians?"

Longarm didn't waste any breath trying to calm her fears or pay any attention to the way her nubile body was pressed against his side. He tore his arm loose from her grasp and gave her a hard shove that sent her reeling to the floor again. Just in time, too, because the next instant a bullet smashed through the window, showering glass around them.

Longarm's cheek stung where a flying splinter from the shattered window had cut it. He crouched lower and looked for an opportunity to return the fire. The train had come to a stop just beyond a bend in the tracks. The fact that it had slowed down somewhat to take the curve might have kept it from derailing. A rocky ridge shouldered down from the north. Smoke drifted from behind some of the boulders scattered on that ridge, so Longarm knew that the men who had stopped the train were concealed behind the big rocks.

Some of them, anyway. More shots came from the front of the train. Gunmen were probably trying to take over the locomotive. The tracks must have been torn up or blocked somehow, forcing the train to come to a sudden halt, and then gun-throwers had rushed forward out of hiding and attacked the cab while more bushwhackers peppered the rest of the cars from the ridge. It all made for a large, well-coordinated assault.

Which meant he was up against professionals, more than likely, Longarm thought grimly, and considerably outnumbered to boot. Of course, he wasn't the only one on the train capable of putting up a fight. The crew was tough, and many of the passengers would be armed, too.

The boulders on the ridge were out of range for his handgun. Thoughts raced through his mind. He could head for the front of the train and try to help defend the locomotive, but that would leave Stockton and his bunch unprotected at the rear of the train. He had no way of knowing the motives of the gang outside. They might be gunmen hired by Lucius Thorne to stop the train, or they might be bandits with nothing more on their minds than looting the express car and robbing the passengers. The one thing he was sure of was that the attackers weren't Indians. Apaches didn't operate this way.

If the gunmen worked for Thorne, they would show up back here sooner or later, Longarm thought. He could prepare for their attack better by getting everyone together in one car, instead of spread out.

Whirling away from the window, he saw the Fords still lying on the floor, Timothy dazed and Millicent sobbing and paralyzed with fright. He bent and grasped Millicent's arm. She was slender and didn't weigh much. Longarm lifted her onto her feet without any trouble. At the same time he prodded Timothy in the side with a booted toe and said sharply, "Get up, old son! Time to get moving."

Timothy pushed himself onto his hands and knees and shook his head groggily. He must have hit his head on the floor when he fell, Longarm thought. After a few seconds, the young man staggered to his feet and said, "What . . . what's going on? Is somebody *shooting* at us?"

"That's right," Longarm said, pushing Millicent at him. "Take your wife and get back in Stockton's private car— *now!*"

Millicent was crying and shaking. Timothy put an arm around her shoulders and said, "Come on, darling. We've got to go."

They stumbled toward the rear door of the car. "Move quick when you cross the platform," Longarm called after them. That would be when they were in the most danger.

He turned toward the front of the train, toward the other special car that had been hooked on in Santa Fe. Dushane was up there, along with Count von Steglitz and Jason Lawlor. He wanted to get them and herd them into Stockton's car as well. He wasn't sure where the Wilcoxes were, but he hoped they were in Stockton's car already, since they hadn't been here with the Fords. Angela would be wherever Stockton was, of course.

Longarm didn't know about Marie, and that doubt caused a cold worm of fear to crawl around in his belly. Marie was probably with her brother, too, but Longarm couldn't be sure of that.

Just as he reached the front door of the car, the rear door of the next car burst open and the three men Longarm sought rushed out of it. Dushane had a pistol in his hand, as did Lawlor. And the count, bringing up the rear, had his shotgun. Longarm waved them on. "Back to

Stockton's car!" he told them. "We'll fort up there!"

Dushane and Lawlor hurried across the platform, but von Steglitz stopped, brought the shotgun to his shoulder, and fired a futile double-barreled blast toward the ridge as he shouted curses in German. The show of resistance didn't accomplish anything except to draw even heavier fire from the hidden riflemen. Slugs sparked and whined off the iron railings of the platform, and von Steglitz suddenly grunted and stumbled as he started toward Longarm. Blood stained the left leg of his trousers where a bullet had caught him.

Longarm reached forward to grab the count's arm and steady him. A slug whipped past his ear. He jerked von Steglitz off the platform and through the door.

"Anybody else in the other car?" Longarm asked.

"No, just us," Lawlor replied. "I'm pretty sure Edward and Claire were back with Grant already."

"Let's go, then."

"I can walk!" von Steglitz protested, but when Longarm let go of his arm, he promptly fell on his face as his wounded leg collapsed under him. Longarm and Lawlor each took an arm and quickly hauled the bulky Prussian to his feet again.

"I'll help him," Lawlor volunteered, and Longarm didn't argue. He covered their rear as the small group hurried through the car.

Stockton was waiting for them as they hustled into the ornate private car. He seemed calm, but his eyes were wide. "Is it Thorne?" he rapped at Longarm.

"How the hell should I know? I ain't seen any of the gunmen yet, and even if I had, I wouldn't know if they were working for Thorne."

"No, of course not." Stockton clutched at Longarm's sleeve. "Have you seen Marie?"

That worm of fear in Longarm's belly turned hairy and sprouted legs. "She ain't back here with you?"

"No, she went forward on the train a little while ago. She took a basket of fruit from our pantry and said she wanted to share it with the children in the coaches."

That was a nice gesture, Longarm thought, but it might wind up getting Marie killed. "Stay here," he said. "I'll go look for her."

Stockton caught at him again. "No! You have to stay here and protect us!"

Disgust made a bad taste in Longarm's mouth. Stockton was talking about leaving his own sister to fend for herself against the men who had stopped the train. And yet, if Thorne was behind the attack, Stockton had a point. The gunmen would converge on this car sooner or later.

But Dushane and Lawlor were armed and ready to fight, and Edward Wilcox might be able to handle the count's shotgun. The Wilcoxes were here; Longarm had seen them huddled on a divan when he came in, along with Timothy and Millicent Ford. On the other side of the car, Angela sat in an armchair, a half-smile on her face, evidently unconcerned about the chaos going on around her. That was because of the drugs coursing through her veins, Longarm thought.

"I won't be gone long," he said to Stockton. "You can put up a fight if you have to."

"Parker, if you leave now"—Stockton's voice shook a little with a mixture of anger and fear—"you're fired!"

"Well, that's just too damned bad," Longarm threw over his shoulder as he went out the door.

He hurried through the now-empty two cars just ahead of Stockton's car. Bullets clawed the air around him every time he crossed one of the platforms. Most of the windows on the north side of the train had been shot out already, and more slugs buzzed through the cars themselves. Longarm moved in a crouch.

He heard guns banging as he reached the next car, the Pullman where he'd had his rendezvous with Marie and been attacked by the two bushwhackers who had wound up dead. The berths converted to sitting compartments during the day, and some of the passengers were at the windows putting up a fight. Longarm moved on through to the next car with its less expensive bench seats. From the sound of what Stockton had said, that was Marie's destination when she left with the basket of fruit.

Sure enough, he spotted her sitting on the floor between two of the benches, holding a terrified little girl in her arms. "Custis!" she called.

Longarm hurried to her side and dropped to a knee. "Are you all right?"

"I'm fine. But you're bleeding!"

Longarm had forgotten about the cut on his cheek from the flying glass. "It's nothing," he said. "Let's get back to your brother's car. I've rounded up the rest of the bunch there."

Marie shook her head and looked at the crying little girl on her lap. "I can't leave, Custis. I'm needed here."

"Damn it—" Longarm started, but he bit back the rest of it. Marie was right. And he might be needed here, too, he thought, instead of back yonder protecting a bunch of pampered rich folks.

But if those were Thorne's men out there, the showdown would come at Stockton's car, and Longarm might be able to get to the bottom of this mess at last. Normally one of the most decisive of men, he was at this moment torn much more than usual in his emotions.

Then he reached out, squeezed Marie's shoulder for a second, and said, "Keep your head down."

She nodded. "I will. You be careful, too, Custis."

Longarm grinned reassuringly at her.

Then he was gone, hurrying back toward the private car at the rear of the train.

# Chapter 23

Instead of running through the other cars as he had before, when he reached the first platform Longarm swung down on the south side of the train. No shots were coming from that direction, so he was able to use the whole bulk of the train itself for cover as he headed toward the rear.

Unfortunately, before he got there a dozen men on horseback came boiling up out of a dry wash about fifty yards south of the tracks and galloped toward Stockton's car.

The barrage of gunfire from the ridge to the north was just a diversion, Longarm realized. Those riflemen hidden behind the boulders were supposed to keep everybody on the train pinned down and busy while this smaller band of raiders carried out a quick strike on Stockton's private car.

Longarm brought up the Colt and fired. One of the riders jerked and swayed in the saddle but managed to stay on his horse. The others blasted shots back at Longarm, who was forced to duck into the gap between cars. It was a good thing the tracks were blocked, he thought as he remembered what the would-be assassin from the night before had looked like after falling under the train.

If the cars started rolling now, Longarm would have been in a bad fix.

Not that he was in clover or anything, he thought wryly as slugs ricocheted around him.

He ducked under the coupling and started crawling along the roadbed toward the rear of the train. He had gone from the top to the bottom in less than twenty-four hours, he told himself with a taut grin. Moving as fast as possible, he scurried along underneath the car.

The shots got louder as the raiders closed in on the train. Longarm crawled under another coupling. He wasn't far from Stockton's car now, but he didn't know if he could get there in time. The defenders would be heavily outnumbered and outgunned. But if they could hold off the bushwhackers until Longarm got in position to launch a flank attack . . .

A shotgun boomed as he reached the front of Stockton's car. Rolling out from under the train, Longarm surged to his feet and saw a couple of men holding the horses. That meant the raiders had already forced their way inside the car. A woman screamed as guns racketed.

The horse holders spotted Longarm and jerked iron. The big lawman fired first and sent one of the men staggering backward. The man stayed on his feet and hung on stubbornly to the reins, however, even though the horses were spooked by the shooting and danced around skittishly. The other man blazed away at Longarm, forcing him to drop to a knee. The horses jumped around even more, blocking Longarm's view of the two men.

The screaming got louder and shriller as gunmen backed onto the rear platform, firing into the car as they retreated. A couple of the men weren't shooting, because they had their hands full keeping Angela Boothe corralled. Fear must have dispelled that drugged haze from her brain, because she certainly fought and caterwauled like she knew she was being kidnapped. Longarm couldn't risk a shot in that direction for fear of hitting her.

The men holding her practically threw her off the platform. Some of the gunnies who had already jumped down grabbed her and slung her over the back of a horse. The air was choked with blinding clouds of dust. Longarm stabbed a shot at one of the raiders and saw the man go down, but renewed firing in his direction from the others made him sprawl on the cinders of the roadbed.

Then the men who were still able to ride were in the saddle and whirling their horses. One of them grabbed his shoulder as a slug fired from inside the car creased him. From his position on the ground, Longarm brought down another of the men. But the others were riding hard now, kicking their horses into gallops that carried them back toward the draw where they had been hidden earlier.

They took Angela with them.

There must have been some sort of signal passed between the groups, because the firing from the ridge dwindled as the riflemen hidden up there began to withdraw. Likewise, the men who had kept the engineer and the firemen pinned down in the cab of the locomotive pulled back, too. Longarm couldn't see them, but he heard the firing dying down and knew what it meant.

The bushwhackers had gotten what they wanted: Angela Boothe.

There had been quite a battle inside the car, Longarm saw a moment later when he entered it. Bullets had ripped the fancy upholstery on the furniture and busted bottles behind the bar. A couple of chairs were overturned. Dushane knelt next to Grant Stockton, who lay unmoving on the floor. Longarm couldn't tell at a glance how badly Stockton was hurt. Edward Wilcox sat on the floor with his back propped against a wall. Blood stained his shirt as his wife fussed over him. Millicent Ford was down, too, but judging by the way her husband knelt beside her chafing her wrists, she must have just fainted. Jason Lawlor had a bullet burn on his cheek but seemed unharmed otherwise. His face was pale and taut with anger. Count von Steglitz hadn't been hit again, but he was still incapacitated by the leg wound he had received earlier.

Longarm joined Dushane beside Stockton. "How bad is he hit?" He saw a bloody furrow on the side of Stockton's head.

"Just creased, I believe," Dushane said. "He should come around in a moment."

True to Dushane's prediction, only a few more moments passed before Stockton began to stir. He groaned, and his eyes flickered open. Suddenly he bolted upright, crying in a ragged voice, "Angela!"

Dushane caught hold of his shoulders. "Name of a name, *mon ami*, you must not excite yourself. Head wounds are dangerous things, even the shallow ones."

Stockton looked around wildly. "Angela!" he said again. "They had Angela! They can't have taken her—"

"They got away with her, all right," Longarm said. "But just because they took her don't mean they can keep her."

Stockton gripped his arm. "You've got to go after her!" he said. "We have to get her back! We have to!"

Longarm nodded and said, "That's just what I figure on doing."

By the time twenty minutes had passed, Longarm had a handle on the situation. Edward Wilcox was the most seriously injured of the group with a wound in his side, but he would probably be all right once he received some medical attention when the train got to Flagstaff. The train crew and some of the male passengers were hard at work clearing away the boulders that had been rolled onto the tracks to stop the locomotive. The telegraph wires on the poles alongside the railroad had been cut, so nobody could shinny up a pole and wire into town for help.

Longarm found the conductor and asked, "Are there any horses in the freight cars?"

"As a matter of fact, we have an actual stable car on this train, and there are eight horses being carried in it," the conductor replied.

Longarm nodded. "Good. I'll need six of 'em."

The conductor's eyes widened in surprise. "But you can't just take those horses!" he exclaimed. "They're not yours."

"Remember our talk last night?" Longarm asked in a low-pitched voice, although it was doubtful anyone would overhear him in the commotion that the bushwhackers had left behind them. "About the Justice Department?"

The conductor nodded slowly. "Well, I suppose if it's government business . . . You'll be careful with those mounts, though, won't you? They're the railroad's responsibility."

"I'll bring 'em back safe and sound if I can," Longarm promised.

Once that had been arranged, he strode back to Stockton's car, where he found Marie winding a bandage around her brother's bullet-creased head.

"I'm going after them," Longarm announced. "Reckon I can use all the help I can get."

"I'll go with you," Stockton said without hesitation. "We have to rescue Angela."

"But, Grant, you're hurt!" Marie protested. "You can't—"

"You don't understand," Stockton grated. "I don't have any choice."

Now that was interesting, Longarm thought. Stockton was acting like Angela's safety was a matter of his own life and death. She was more than just his mistress, that was for sure.

Jason Lawlor was reloading his pistol. He snapped the cylinder closed and said, "I'll go along, Parker."

"As will I," Dushane declared.

That made four of them. Long odds against an entire gang of killers, but probably the best he was going to get, Longarm told himself.

Timothy Ford spoke up. "I . . . I'll go, too," he said.

Millicent, who had come around from her faint, said, "No, absolutely not. You'll just get yourself killed, Timothy."

"But those men kidnapped Miss Boothe. We have to save her."

"Let Parker and the others go after her," Millicent insisted.

A stubborn look came over Timothy's face as he shook his head. "I'm sorry, Millie, but I've got to do this." He looked at Longarm. "If you'll help me find a gun, Mr. Parker, I'll be glad to go with you."

Longarm didn't know how much help the youngster would be, but at least Timothy would be one more warm body who could pull the trigger of a gun. Longarm nodded. "I'm obliged. We'll come up with a gun for you."

"You're all insane!" Millicent cried. "You're risking your lives for some . . . some English trollop!"

"Angela is more than that, Millicent," Stockton said quietly, "and you know it." He faced Longarm. "We'll be ready to ride whenever you say, Parker."

"Better not waste any more time, then," Longarm said. "They've already got a good lead on us."

# Chapter 24

Out of the men who went with Longarm, both Grant Stockton and Timothy Ford sat a saddle fairly well, having ridden in the parks back in Philadelphia. Lawlor had been on a horse before but wasn't as confident as the two younger men. Dushane was game, but by the way he bounced in the saddle, Longarm knew the Frenchman was going to be mighty sore by the next day.

They had scrounged up Winchesters for everyone, and each man carried a pistol as well. If the gang that had stopped the train stayed together, the rescuers would be outnumbered by four or five to one. . . . Terrible odds, but there was nothing that could be done about it. They would have to rely on stealth and guile, Longarm thought.

And siding him in that effort would be a foreigner and three greenhorns from back east.

Well, as the Indians said, it was a good day to die.

Longarm picked up the gang's trail in the dry wash. They hadn't gone to any trouble to conceal their tracks, which showed how confident they were. Stockton rode beside Longarm while the other three strung out behind, with Dushane bringing up the rear. That was all right with Longarm. He knew from experience that although Dushane might not be much of a horseman, the fella from Paris was a good shot and coolheaded under fire.

"Will we be able to catch up to them?" Stockton asked.

"We stand a good chance of it," Longarm told him. "We can travel a little faster than a big bunch like that, and they've got the girl with them, too, although they won't let that slow them down much." He looked over at Stockton. "Unless they decide she's too much trouble and get rid of her."

Stockton shook his head. "They won't do that. They need her alive and in good shape."

"Care to tell me how come you're so sure of that?"

"Just believe it," Stockton said curtly.

Longarm didn't press the issue. He could find out later just why Angela Boothe was so all-fired important . . . assuming, of course, that they were able to get her away from the gang and they all lived through it.

"The inside of that railroad car looked like there'd been a battle fought there," he commented as he rode along. His eyes were constantly moving, darting from the tracks they were following to the surrounding landscape, alert for any sign of an ambush. They were headed for Diablo Canyon, and if the pursuit continued beyond that, the Mogollon Rim. Mighty rugged territory, any way you looked at it, Longarm thought, and prime country for a trap.

"Yes, it was pretty bad in there for a few moments," Stockton agreed. "We were lucky no one was killed or seriously wounded. I think those gunmen were trying to be careful, though, because they didn't want to hurt Angela. Once they had their hands on her, they didn't care about us anymore. They just wanted to get out with their prize."

"I thought you said Thorne wanted you dead."

"I'm sure Lucius Thorne wouldn't be upset if I were killed," Stockton said. "On the other hand, as long as Angela is his prisoner, he has the upper hand, and he knows it. He's an arrogant bastard. He probably thinks I'm too petty a threat to worry about anymore." Stockton's voice hardened. "He's going to find out just how wrong he is."

Longarm didn't ask any more questions for the moment, although he was as curious as ever why Angela Boothe was so important.

This part of Arizona Territory wasn't nearly as hot as it got down along the border, but even at these elevations, the sun was pretty warm at midday. Dushane and Lawlor had started out wearing coats, but by noon they took them off and rolled them up, tying them behind their saddles. Longarm was the only one wearing a hat, and he was grateful for the shade that the wide-brimmed Stetson provided as they rode along the rim of Diablo Canyon. Lawlor took out a handkerchief and mopped sweat off his flushed face.

"Are we still on the right trail?" he asked irritably.

"Those are the tracks we've been following since we left the railroad," Longarm said. He reined in. "But there's something mighty interesting."

The other riders came to a halt as well. "What is it?" Stockton asked.

Longarm pointed to the ground. It was pretty hard and dry along here and didn't take tracks well, but he was an old hand at following dim trails. "The bunch split up here," he said. "Some of 'em cut west while most of them kept on south toward the Mogollon Rim."

"Which ones have Angela with them?" Stockton asked, an edge of panic creeping into his voice. "Which ones do we follow?"

"That's a mighty good question. Ain't no way to tell which bunch has the gal. We can split up and try to follow both trails, and hope that we spot some sign of her."

Stockton shook his head. "You're the only one who really knows what he's doing out here, Parker. If we split up, the group that isn't with you will probably get lost."

"That's pretty much what I thought. Reckon you'll just have to take a chance." One thing occurred to Longarm that might make the decision easier. "Thorne will want Angela brought to him, right?"

Stockton seized on that hope, saying eagerly, "That's right. He has a ranch in California, in the hills just north of Los Angeles. That's where we were going to meet him."

"It's a hell of a long, hard ride down to Phoenix from here," Longarm said, explaining his thinking. "They could catch the Southern Pacific there. But if the bunch that headed west circles around Hutch Mountain and then goes north again, they can link up with the Santa Fe at Williams. That'd be the quickest way to get the girl to California."

"That must be what they're doing," Stockton said excitedly. "I know Thorne. He's an impatient man. He'll want Angela delivered to him as soon as possible."

"Then chances are she's with the bunch that went west," Longarm said. "But you got to realize, it's a gamble either way."

"I say we risk it," Lawlor put in. "Like Grant said, we can't afford to split up."

"This sounds reasonable to me as well," Dushane weighed in.

Timothy Ford shrugged. "I'll go along with what everybody thinks is best."

"West it is, then," Stockton said. "And we'd better not waste any more time."

Longarm agreed with that. He set a fast pace as they rode out on the trail of the men who had gone west.

Just as he expected, after a while the tracks curved back to the north toward the town of Williams. By the time the gang got there, the same train that they had stolen Angela off of would be headed in that direction. The railroad had to keep to its schedule as much as possible, so the train would have dropped off Stockton's three cars in Flagstaff. Stockton had made that arrangement with the conductor before the group of would-be rescuers rode away. The kidnappers could board the train in Williams and ride on to deliver Angela in California. They would have to make sure she kept quiet and cooperated, and they might even try to disguise her. That would be easy enough to do if she feared for her life.

It was a neat trick the gang had planned, Longarm thought. He and his companions had to catch up to them before they reached Williams in order to spoil those plans.

And of course, it was still possible that they were wrong, that Angela Boothe was in the hands of the men who had ridden south. If that was the case, she would be long gone before they could ever catch up to her.

Longarm had seen to it that they brought a little food with them from the train, some bread and fruit. They ate in the saddle, pausing only to let the horses drink at an occasional creek and rest for a few minutes. The afternoon wore on, with Hutch Mountain rising to the right, Williams Mountain to the left, and Humphreys Peak, the highest mountain in the territory, off to the northeast. Longarm knew they ought to be getting to the town of Williams soon.

It was late afternoon when he heard the distant whistle of a train. That would be the westbound approaching the town. Only the fact that it had taken quite a while to clear the tracks east of Flagstaff had given them the chance to reach Williams in time. Without that delay, the train would have already passed through on its way to California.

"Come on," Longarm called to the others as he heeled his horse into a faster pace. "We got to hurry."

The horses were tired, but they were range-bred animals with an inner core of strength and stamina. They responded valiantly when the men called on them for more speed. A few minutes later the group rode out of a wash and came in sight of the town. Longarm saw puffs of smoke and steam rising from the locomotive where it was stopped at the depot. They were in time. The train hadn't pulled out yet.

A much more experienced rider, Longarm drew ahead of the others as he galloped his mount toward the depot. Stockton and the rest tried their best to keep up.

The station was on the southern edge of town, so Longarm was able to reach it without having to ride through the settlement itself. He raced to the end of the platform and was out of the saddle before his horse came to a full stop. As he bounded up the steps, he scanned the scattering of people on the platform. He spotted several hardfaced men and a woman in a long dress and sunbonnet heading toward the entrance of one of the cars.

"Angela!" he shouted.

The woman in the bonnet jerked her head around, and for a second Longarm peered into the wide, terrified eyes of Angela Boothe. The next instant, one of the men with her leaped in front of her, bringing up a gun. The weapon in his hand spurted flame as he fired at the onrushing lawman.

151

# Chapter 25

Longarm darted to the side as the gun-thrower fired. The slug buzzed past his head like an angry hornet. He palmed out his Colt as the innocent bystanders on the depot platform yelled in alarm and scurried to get out of the line of fire.

There were six of the kidnappers. Two of them tried to hustle a suddenly struggling Angela onto the train while the other three joined the first one who had taken a shot at Longarm. The big lawman darted behind a cart full of baggage that had been abandoned by the porter when the gunfire had started. Bullets thudded into the bags as Longarm crouched there. He snapped a shot at the gunmen and was rewarded by the sight of one of them staggering from a bullet-torn thigh.

There were still three of them pouring lead at Longarm, though, and that was enough to keep him pinned down.

Or at least it would have been if Timothy Ford hadn't come running onto the platform, shouting excitedly and blazing away with the gun in his hand. His shots went wild, but they came close enough to distract the gunmen. A couple of the men turned to deal with this new threat, and that gave Longarm the chance to fire again and drive a bullet into one man's midsection.

As that gunnie crumpled and fell onto the platform, Stockton, Lawlor, and Dushane all arrived on the scene and began firing. Longarm left them to deal with the remaining gunmen and leaped out from behind the baggage cart. He had just seen Angela forced into one of the cars by the two men holding her. The steps leading up to another car were close at hand. Longarm took them in a couple of bounds and ran into the car.

The passengers already on board saw the gun in his hand and got out of the way as he ran toward the front of the train. He realized that he was in the same Pullman car where he and Marie had spent the previous night in each other's arms. That seemed like days in the past, rather than mere hours. Longarm hurried through the car and into the next one.

One of the kidnappers burst in the door at the far end and opened fire. A slug chewed splinters from the top of the bench next to Longarm. He triggered two fast shots and saw the gunman thrown backward by the crashing impact of the leaden slugs.

That left just one man with Angela, but Longarm didn't know where they were. As he hurdled the fallen body of the man he had just shot and ran into the next car, he didn't see any sign of them. Then one of the men in the coach realized who Longarm must be looking for and said, "They got back off, mister! They went straight through and out the other side!"

So Angela and her captor were on the south side of the train now. Longarm reached the front platform and swung down, casting quick glances in both directions along the string of cars. He caught sight of his quarry up by the locomotive. The man hurried Angela along, one hand gripping her arm while the other held a revolver.

"Hold it!" Longarm shouted after them.

The man twisted and stabbed a shot at him. The bullet whined off a brass fitting on the car next to Longarm. He held his fire for fear of hitting Angela and went after them at a run. He figured the kidnapper was trying to reach the cab of the locomotive. The engine had steam up; the gunman probably hoped to force the engineer to pull out of the station at gunpoint. Longarm couldn't let that happen. If the train got away, he wouldn't have any way of catching it.

The cinders of the roadbed crunched under his booted feet as he sprinted toward the front of the train. He weaved as the kidnapper snapped another shot at him, missing again. Angela struggled with the man, trying to pull away from his grip, but he was too strong for her. He dragged her along, moving so fast that her feet barely touched the ground.

They ran past the coal tender and reached the locomotive. Longarm saw the engineer lean down out of the cab and heard him yell, "Hey! What in tarnation—"

The kidnapper fired up at him, brutally smashing a slug through the body of the surprised engineer. The trainman clutched at his chest and toppled out of the cab, landing on the ground next to the locomotive and rolling over a couple of times.

Practically slinging Angela ahead of him, the gunman climbed up into the cab. Longarm bit back a curse. The man must have had some experience with engines and planned to take the controls himself, he thought.

Sure enough, the next moment the train began to move. Steam hissed and roared and the drivers clanked on the rails as they sought purchase. The train picked up speed. Longarm jammed his Colt back in its holster and reached up for the grab iron at the back of a freight car as it moved past him.

He was jerked off his feet as the train moved faster

154

and faster. Getting a second hand on the iron, he hauled himself up until he could reach the rungs of the ladder at the rear of the car. Damned if he wasn't about to climb on top of the blasted train again, he thought as he clambered up the ladder.

Up in the cab, the kidnapper wouldn't have been able to see him climbing onto the freight car. The bastard probably thought he had made a clean getaway . . . although how he figured he was going to make it all the way to Los Angeles with a stolen train, Longarm didn't have a clue. Probably the kidnapper intended to abandon the train and find some other way to get Angela to California when he had left all the pursuers far behind.

Well, here was one pursuer who wasn't getting left behind, Longarm thought as he pulled himself on top of the freight car.

He moved forward on hands and knees, staying low so that the kidnapper would be less likely to notice him if he glanced back along the train. He had to come up into a crouch to leap to the next car, but then he went back to crawling. Slowly, he worked his way toward the locomotive.

Longarm knew how loud it was in the cab. He wasn't worried about the kidnapper hearing his approach. When he reached the coal tender, he lowered himself by his hands and dropped onto the mound of greasy black rocks. He moved forward a little more and saw the kidnapper standing at the controls, right hand on the throttle while his left held a gun on Angela, who sat huddled in a corner of the cab.

It would be an easy shot from here, but the gunman's reflexes might cause him to squeeze the trigger when the bullet struck him, and at that range his shot would be almost certain to hit Angela. Longarm couldn't risk it. He moved closer and came up in a crouch, poised for a leap down into the cab.

Angela glanced up, saw him, and her suddenly widening eyes gave him away. The gunman noticed her reaction, cursed, and started to turn.

Longarm launched himself into the air.

He reached for the wrist of the kidnapper's gun hand and grabbed it as he crashed into the man. Longarm's momentum carried them both ahead so that they crashed against the controls. The train sped up as the throttle was shoved forward by the impact. The gunman threw a punch that caught Longarm on the jaw and rocked his head back. Longarm's senses reeled for a second, but he hung on desperately and slammed his opponent's gun hand against the front of the cab. The impact knocked the revolver loose. It clattered to the floor.

Longarm sensed the kidnapper's knee coming up toward his groin and twisted aside to take the blow on his hip. He got a hand on the man's neck and hung on tight, using his weight to push the man back and smash his head against the front of the cab. The kidnapper seemed to be weakening, but that just made him all the more desperate. With an incoherent shout, he tore free from Longarm's grasp and swung two swift punches that knocked the lawman backward.

Longarm caught his balance as he fell against the coal tender. The kidnapper lunged at him, but Angela thrust out a leg and tripped him. The man cursed as he stumbled forward. Longarm closed the gunman's mouth with a roundhouse right that knocked him halfway out of the cab. The kidnapper caught himself just in time.

But before he could do anything else, a gun roared. Blood flew from the kidnapper's chest as the bullet crashed into him. He was driven backward, and this time he had no chance to save himself. He flew out of the cab and soared through the air before slamming into the ground. The rolling impact threw up a cloud of dust that

156

instantly fell behind as the train continued speeding along the tracks.

Longarm looked down at Angela and saw the tendril of smoke curling from the barrel of the gun she clutched in both hands. She had picked up the revolver that the kidnapper had dropped, and at this range it had been difficult for her to miss. She hadn't.

Longarm wasted only a second on that, then leaped to the controls and began to ease back the throttle. The train was really high-balling along, but luckily this was a fairly straight stretch of track and it hadn't been in danger of coming off. That wouldn't have been true for much longer, though, as Longarm saw a bend only a couple of hundred yards ahead. He slowed the engine until the train finally came to a stop just short of the bend.

"I . . . I killed him," Angela wailed above the lowering rumble of the engine.

"Damn straight," Longarm told her. "And there ain't nobody going to blame you for it, neither."

He figured they had come four or five miles since leaving the depot at Williams. By now a posse was probably galloping after them, led by Stockton or one of the other men.

Longarm was no engineer, but he knew enough about the controls to be able to start the train backing toward town. He kept the speed pretty slow. The frightened passengers had to be wondering what the hell was going on, but they would find out soon enough.

Considering that many of those folks had probably been through the attack on the other side of Flagstaff, they had to be getting tired of being caught in the middle of all these gun battles. One thing was certain, Longarm thought. This train trip had been a mite more exciting than they had expected when they bought their tickets.

# Chapter 26

In an effort to make her harder to recognize, the kidnappers had cut Angela's long blond hair, hacking it off short with a Bowie knife. They'd also had the long dress and the sunbonnet with them, so that they could dress her like a sodbuster's wife. It probably would have worked if not for the quick actions of Longarm and the men who had come on the rescue mission with him.

Just as he expected, a posse met the train before it got back to Williams. Longarm spotted Grant Stockton riding with the leaders of the group and waved at him from the cab. Angela stood up and waved as well to let Stockton know that she wasn't hurt. The rancher turned his horse, rode alongside the cab, and called, "Angela! Angela, are you all right?"

She cupped her hands around her mouth and shouted back, "I'm fine!"

A look of immense relief came over Stockton's face. He didn't look much like a wealthy gentleman from back east anymore. His clothes were coated with trail dust, and his features showed the strain of the long ride. He summoned up a smile, though, when he was sure that Angela hadn't been harmed.

At that moment, Longarm almost liked Stockton. Almost . . . but then he remembered how Stockton had smuggled Angela out of Kansas City, arranged with the three toughs to murder anyone who came looking for her, and kept her drugged for the past few weeks. The gent was up to no good, that was certain, and Longarm hoped it wouldn't be much longer before he discovered the details of the nefarious game Stockton was playing.

He didn't see Dushane, Lawlor, or Timothy Ford with the posse and hoped that the men hadn't been killed or wounded in that shootout with the other kidnappers on the platform. He might not have been able to rescue Angela if they hadn't come along when they did, while he was pinned down behind that baggage cart.

A few minutes later the train backed into the depot, and Longarm eased it to a stop alongside the platform. He swung down from the cab and turned to help Angela, but before he could, Stockton was there beside him, reaching up for her.

Longarm stepped back, letting Stockton help her. Stockton drew her into his arms and hugged her tightly, stroking her now-short hair.

Longarm saw Dushane, Lawlor, and Timothy Ford coming along the platform toward him. Timothy had a bloodstained bandage around his left arm. Millicent was going to have a fit over that, Longarm thought. Lawlor seemed to be unhurt, and though Dushane was limping, Longarm thought it was from the long ride, not because of any wound.

"You have returned in triumph, *M'sieur* Parker," Dushane said. "The young lady, she is unharmed, no?"

"She is unharmed, yes," Longarm said. "Other than having her hair chopped off, and I reckon she'll get over that just fine. What happened to those other fellas who grabbed her?"

Lawlor nodded toward some canvas-shrouded shapes

159

farther along the platform. "They're waiting for the undertaker," he said. "They put up a pretty good fight, but a couple of deputies from the town showed up and pitched in on our side. They'd already had a wire from Flagstaff about what was going on."

"I got shot!" Timothy put in.

Longarm grinned at him. "Reckon you're going to live?"

"Oh, I think so. The doctor who tended to my wound said I just got nicked. It hurt like blazes when it happened, but it's not too bad now." The young man moved his arm. "Just a little stiff and sore."

Longarm clapped a hand on the shoulder of Timothy's uninjured arm. "Reckon you can count that bandage as a badge of honor. Without the help you fellas gave me, we might not have gotten Miss Boothe back safe and sound."

"We couldn't let those bastards get away with her," Lawlor growled.

Longarm wondered just how much Lawlor and the others knew about what was going on. Were they aware that Stockton was drugging Angela? Did they know about the attempt on Longarm's life back in Kansas City? Were they just as guilty as Stockton . . . whatever Stockton was actually guilty of?

More unanswered questions, Longarm thought.

But maybe the answers were waiting in California.

The next westbound train wasn't due for two days, so the group had to wait in Williams for that time. Stockton rented rooms for all of them in the town's only decent hotel. Angela had her own room, for appearance's sake, but Longarm knew she didn't stay in it. Stockton kept her in his room, clearly not wanting to let her out of his sight again.

Longarm wondered if Stockton had brought any of that "special" brandy along with him to keep her under his control. When he saw the dreamy look in Angela's eyes at supper that first night, he knew the answer. Stockton had gone right back to drugging her.

He wished he'd had a chance to talk with her before Stockton got her under his spell again, but things had been too hectic while they were together in the cab of the locomotive.

Stockton visited the local telegraph office and sent a wire to Lucius Thorne. "Have to let him know that we've been delayed, but that we still plan to meet him at his ranch," Stockton explained.

And in the process, Stockton was rubbing Thorne's nose in it that the attempt to kidnap Angela had failed, Longarm thought. Thorne would have gotten that idea when his men didn't show up with her, but Stockton wanted his enemy to know about it sooner.

Stockton wired Flagstaff, too, to let Marie and the others know what had happened. A couple of days later the next westbound train rolled into the Williams depot, bringing with it Stockton's private car and the other two special cars, all of which had been hooked on in Flagstaff. Marie was waiting on the front platform of Stockton's car, along with Millicent Ford and Count von Steglitz, who leaned on a silver-headed cane.

Millicent leaped down from the steps while the train was still coming to a stop and hugged her husband. "Timothy!" she cried. "Thank God you're all right!" She pulled back from him and stared at the black silk sling which supported his left arm. "But you're hurt!"

"It's nothing," Timothy said with a proud grin. "I'll be fine."

Marie stepped down to the platform and embraced her brother, then Angela. Finally she turned to Longarm and touched his hand. "Custis . . ." she said. "I was worried about you."

"No need to worry," Longarm told her with a grin. "I'm right as rain."

She squeezed his hand. "Yes, I can see that."

Longarm learned quickly that Edward and Claire Wilcox were in one of the special cars. The doctor in Flagstaff had advised Wilcox not to continue the trip but to stay there and recuperate from his wound, but Wilcox had insisted on leaving when the others did, and of course his wife had come along. He spent most of his time in his compartment, though, resting.

The rescue party hadn't taken any baggage with them when they left the train east of Flagstaff, so all their things were still on board. The stop in Williams didn't take long. A short time later, the train was rolling west once more, again with a full complement of passengers in the three extra cars.

Longarm dined in Stockton's car with the others that evening, and as he looked around he saw that they were a more battered bunch than they had been when they left Santa Fe. Wilcox, Timothy Ford, and von Steglitz were all wounded, and Pierre Dushane was still very sore from the horseback ride. The Frenchman was bearing up under the discomfort gamely, however, joking that he would never get near a horse again unless it was pulling a carriage.

Afterwards, Longarm stepped out onto the platform to smoke a cheroot. Not surprisingly, Marie joined him. She moved easily into his arms and lifted her face to his for a kiss. Her lips opened and her tongue stroked boldly into Longarm's mouth. Her body molded itself to his so that he felt every sensuous, exciting curve. He reacted strongly, hardening so that his shaft prodded against her soft belly.

She broke the kiss and rested her head against his chest. "I was so afraid after you rode off like that," she whispered. "I thought I'd never see you again."

162

"I'm a pretty tough hombre," he said, a hint of self-mockery in his voice. "I can take care of myself."

"I know you can. And you can take care of me, too. In fact, I happen to know there's a Pullman berth in the next car that's unoccupied, just like on the other train. . . ."

Longarm laughed. "I reckon I can count on you to stay informed about things like that."

"You certainly can." She gave him a teasing smile. "I'll see you up there in, say, fifteen minutes?"

"No lace handkerchief this time?"

"No, and no ambush, either. Just come to the third compartment on the left."

Longarm nodded. "I'll be there."

He was, and just as Marie had predicted, there was no ambush.

Unless, of course, Longarm reflected, you wanted to count being grabbed by a beautiful naked lady and forced to make love to her for a couple of hours. Being ambushed like that was just fine with him.

# Chapter 27

The sky over Los Angeles and the Santa Monica Mountains to the north was a beautiful, crystal-clear blue when the train pulled into the station. A warm ocean breeze blew in from the Pacific as the passengers disembarked. Longarm liked Los Angeles. In the past few years, since the railroads had reached it, it had grown from a sleepy little farming community nestled in a cup formed by the sea and the mountains into a bustling town with more than ten thousand residents. Given the fact that the weather was nice here year-round, and the land was good, though a little dry, Longarm figured the place would continue to grow. If anybody ever figured out a way to improve the water supply, folks would flock here from all over, more than likely.

Stockton had wired ahead and had carriages waiting at the station to take them to the hotel where they would be staying. It was a sprawling adobe building, with red-tiled roofs on its various wings, that resembled one of the many old Spanish missions that dotted the landscape here in Southern California.

Longarm's room had a thick rug on the floor and a heavy-framed bed with a thick mattress. The thought crossed his mind that it would be mighty enjoyable to romp on that mattress with Marie Stockton, but more than likely that would have to wait.

A short time after they arrived at the hotel, a man showed up with a message for Grant Stockton. Longarm was in Stockton's suite when the knock came. Stockton started toward the door, but Longarm motioned him back. He went to answer the knock instead, and his hand rested on the butt of his gun as he swung the door open.

The man who stood there was tall and cadaverous-looking, a Mexican with a hooked nose and a mostly bald head. He held his sombrero in his hands and nodded to Longarm. "I seek *Señor* Stockton."

The visitor wore range clothes and was probably a vaquero. He packed a gun on his hip but made no move toward it. Longarm stepped back and said, "Come in, hombre . . . but don't try anything funny."

"I give you my word I will not, *señor.*"

The suite had two bedrooms. Stockton had hustled Angela into one of them after Longarm went to the door. Now he stepped forward and said, "I'm Stockton. Do you have a message from Lucius Thorne?"

The Mexican nodded his skull-like head. "*Si, señor.* I am Ramón, *Señor* Thorne's *segundo.* He wishes me to tell you that he would be honored if you and your friends would have dinner with him this evening at his ranch. He will send carriages for you at eight o'clock."

"Please tell *Señor* Thorne that we accept his kind invitation," Stockton replied smoothly. "We will be ready."

Ramón bowed in acknowledgment of the message and backed out of the suite. Longarm was glad to see him go. The hombre had looked a mite too much like a walking corpse.

He turned to Stockton and said, "I reckon you're going to want me to go along this evening?"

"Of course. But it's time we had a little talk, Parker.

You're going to see some things tonight that are a bit . . . unusual. Are you sure you're prepared for that?"

Longarm shrugged. "You're paying me good wages to be prepared for just about anything, boss."

"Yes, and you certainly came through when I needed you the most, when Thorne's men kidnapped Angela."

"You sure you want to waltz right into the fella's house, what with all the bad blood between you?"

"There's nothing to worry about now," Stockton said firmly. "Thorne knows that I still have the upper hand."

"That didn't stop him from trying to grab the gal before," Longarm pointed out.

"And that's why you're going along, Parker. Just in case Thorne makes one final, foolish play. . . . Not that it would do him any good. After tonight . . ." Stockton stopped and shook his head. "Let's just say that after tonight, everything will be different. Everything."

Longarm didn't much like the sound of that.


"*M'sieur* Delacroix, I'm sure you'll understand that my friends and I have some personal business to take care of this evening. We'll see you again tomorrow, of course."

Stockton spoke suavely to Pierre Dushane as they stood in the hotel bar sipping drinks. Longarm was next to Stockton, keeping an eye on things.

Dushane nodded and said, "*Certainement, M'sieur* Stockton. You have been most kind to allow me to accompany you thus far. I have no wish to intrude on personal matters."

"I appreciate that," Stockton said.

The other members of the group were in the lobby, waiting for the carriages that Lucius Thorne was sending to take them to his ranch. Edward Wilcox, though pale and weak from his wound, had insisted on going along. The fact that all of them were going to Thorne's ranch

166

told Longarm that they all knew about Stockton's plan, whatever it was.

Except for Marie, who was puzzled and had confided as much quietly to Longarm a few minutes earlier. "I reckon your brother knows what he's doing," Longarm had said to her.

"I'm not sure," Marie had replied with a worried frown on her face. "I had been traveling in Europe until about six months ago, and when I got back, Grant was . . . different somehow than he was when I left. I'm worried about him, Custis."

"No need to worry," Longarm had assured her. "I'll be right there to take care of any trouble."

But he had some concerns of his own, he reflected now. He sensed that everything was coming to a head, and he wasn't going to be a bit surprised if the showdown took place tonight at Thorne's ranch. When that happened, he would probably have to arrest Grant Stockton. Afterwards, Marie would likely hate him. But Stockton had to answer to the law for his crimes, even though Longarm wasn't completely sure yet of the extent of them.

Stockton started to return to the lobby after talking to Dushane, but Longarm hung back. "I'll be right there," he told Stockton. "Want to buy some cigars." There was a humidor of cheroots at the end of the bar.

Stockton nodded and went on out. As Longarm took several cigars from the humidor, he said in a low voice to Dushane, "I reckon something's going to happen out at Thorne's place tonight."

"The showdown, as you Americans say?" Dushane murmured, echoing Longarm's thought.

"That's right. Think you can get your hands on a horse and follow us out there?"

Dushane grimaced. "You mean I must ride one of those infernal beasts again?"

"Well, you might be able to rent a buggy," Longarm

said. "It'd be harder to follow us without somebody noticing you, though."

"I will ride the horse," Dushane said grimly. "You may need my help tonight."

"That's just what I was thinking." Longarm looked at the Frenchman. "You're some sort of detective, ain't you?"

"Paris police," Dushane admitted. "I seek the murderer of an old man, a dealer in rarities and antiquities. I believe *M'sieur* Stockton to have been involved in that crime, if in fact he did not order it."

That tied in with something Stockton had told Longarm a few days earlier. "I reckon Thorne's men are likely to blame for the killing. Stockton said they murdered somebody in Paris who was working for him, and they got their hands on something Stockton wanted. Probably one of them rarities or antiquities you mentioned."

"Name of a name!" Dushane muttered. "I believe you are right, Marshal. So I must arrest this man Thorne, as well as Stockton."

"We'll hash out who arrests who later on. For now, just be ready to bust in there if you hear all hell break loose."

"All hell . . . ," Dushane said softly. "Perhaps you are more right than you know."

Longarm frowned at him, unsure what he meant by that, but there was no more time to talk about it. He didn't want Stockton getting suspicious of him at this late date. He tossed the bartender a coin to pay for the cheroots, stuck them in his pocket, and left the bar to join the others in the lobby.

A few minutes later, the spooky-looking vaquero Ramón came in, bowed, and said to Stockton, "The carriages are outside, *señor*. Please come with me."

Stockton looked around at the others. "All right, everyone, let's go." He linked arms with Angela, who looked particularly beautiful tonight, even with her hair cropped off. She had gotten some sort of feathery hat that perched on her head and looked glamorous.

Three carriages were parked on the street outside the hotel. Longarm, Stockton, Angela, and Marie climbed into the first one. The Fords and the Wilcoxes got into the second one, Timothy giving Edward Wilcox a hand. That left Jason Lawlor and Count Otto von Steglitz to ride in the third carriage.

Ramón stepped up to the driver's box of the first carriage and took the reins. He shook them and called out to the team in his gravelly voice, which sounded as if he had just crawled up out of a grave. The horses surged against their harness and pulled the carriage along the hard-packed dirt of the street. The other vehicles followed.

Whatever was waiting for them at Lucius Thorne's ranch, Longarm thought, it wouldn't be long now until they confronted it.

All hell, Longarm had said, and Dushane had agreed.

Despite the warmth of the night, cold fingers played along the big lawman's spine.

# Chapter 28

The road climbed back and forth up the slopes north of town until it reached the spine of the long ridge. From there Longarm could look back down and see the lights of Los Angeles. It was quite a view.

After a while the road turned and descended the northern slope of the mountains into the San Fernando Valley. Longarm knew there were several good-sized ranches up here, many of them having been founded by Californios back in the days of Spanish rule. He supposed Lucius Thorne had either bought one of those ranches or started a spread of his own.

They reached the flats and continued north for a while, until Ramón turned the buggy onto a narrow lane that led off to the west from the main road. Longarm saw the lights of a big ranch house up ahead, surrounded by fruit trees. The three buggies rolled up the long, straight lane that terminated at the house.

"Are you excited, my dear?" Stockton asked Angela. "This is going to be a big night for all of us."

"A big night," Angela agreed in a drowsy voice. Longarm wondered if Stockton had increased the amount of whatever drug he was giving her.

Marie sat beside Longarm. She touched his leg unobtrusively, not in a sensual way but more like she was worried about something. Longarm didn't blame her. He tried to give her a reassuring look, but he couldn't see her very well in the shadows inside the buggy.

Ramón brought the vehicle to a halt, with the other two buggies stopping behind it. Someone in the house must have been watching for their arrival, because the big front door was thrown open and light spilled out into the night. A deep voice boomed out, "Come in, my friends, come in! Welcome to my home!"

That would be the mysterious Lucius Thorne. As Longarm hopped down from the buggy and turned to help Marie disembark, he studied Thorne from the corner of his eye. The man was tall and broad-shouldered, balding on top of his head but with a stiff beard that stuck out belligerently from his chin and reached halfway down his chest. If the beard had been white instead of brown, Thorne would have looked a little like one of those Old Testament prophets. As it was, he looked more like he ought to have his picture on, box of patent medicine cough lozenges.

Longarm put his hands on Marie's trim waist to help her down from the buggy. As he set her on the ground, he hoped again that she wouldn't hate him when this night was over.

Everyone climbed down from the buggies, and Stockton led the way inside the big ranch house with Angela on his arm. Millicent Ford chattered excitedly. An air of anticipation seemed to grip everyone, even the injured Edward Wilcox. When his wife made some comment about him taking it easy, he laughed and said, "Never you worry about me, Claire. Soon I won't have to be concerned about mere physical ailments."

Longarm wondered what in blazes he meant by that. Wilcox sounded almost as if he thought he wasn't going to live through the night. That couldn't be it, though, as happy as he sounded.

The house was opulently furnished, with thick carpets, heavy drapes, and brilliantly polished wood everywhere Longarm looked. It seemed to have a fireplace in every room, and crystal chandeliers hung from all the ceilings. Thorne's home was almost as fancy and elegant as a palace.

"My dear friends," Thorne intoned in his rumbling voice when they were all gathered in a large, beautiful parlor. His deep-set dark eyes didn't look very friendly, though, as he locked gazes with Grant Stockton. Longarm could practically feel the hatred flowing between the two men. Thorne went on, "I'm glad you brought all your associates, Grant."

"We made a pact," Stockton said. "I couldn't leave them behind."

"Of course not." Thorne looked at Longarm. "I'm afraid I haven't made the acquaintance of this tall gentleman, however."

"His name is Custis Long," Stockton said. "He's a deputy United States marshal."

The bold-faced declaration caught Longarm by surprise. Judging by Marie's gasp, she wasn't expecting it, either. She turned to Longarm and asked sharply, "You're a lawman?"

"Yes, ma'am," he drawled, trying not to let it show that Stockton had him a mite off balance. "And your brother there has known it all along, I reckon."

"Certainly," Stockton said. "I wouldn't hire a man just out of the blue like that. But there's an old saying, Marshal Long, about keeping your friends close and your enemies closer. Once you tracked me to Santa Fe, I decided it would be a good idea to have you around so that I could keep an eye on you. And I must admit, you *did* come in

172

handy when poor Angela was kidnapped." Stockton glared for a second at Thorne.

The bearded rancher didn't seem put off by Stockton's enmity. Indeed, Thorne laughed. "Come, come, Grant," he said. "You can't blame a man for trying, especially when the stakes are as high as they are here."

"You lied to me," Marie said quietly but angrily to Longarm. "Why couldn't you just trust me and tell me the truth?"

Stockton answered for Longarm. "Because he came to New Mexico to arrest me . . . didn't you, Marshal?"

"I had it in mind," Longarm admitted, "after I figured out you kidnapped Miss Boothe and tried to have those fellas in Kansas City kill me."

"Kidnapped?" Angela repeated. "Grant didn't kidnap me. He asked me to come with him to his ranch, and I agreed."

"But he told you not to let your aunt and uncle know where you were going," Longarm shot back, "and whether you know it or not, he's been keeping you doped up the whole time."

Angela turned to Stockton. "Grant? I'm confused. None of this makes sense to me."

Stockton patted her shoulder and said easily, "Then you shouldn't worry about it, darling. Let me take care of everything."

"Oh. All right." A broad smile spread across Angela's face.

Marie was still angry with Longarm, but she had begun to realize that something was very wrong here. She said, "Grant, I don't like this. I haven't understood why we came here, or really, most of what you've said and done since I got back from my trip to Europe. What's going on here?"

"The world is about to change, my dear," Stockton

replied smoothly. "I know I should have explained everything to you before now—"

Timothy Ford could no longer contain his excitement. "We're going to be like gods!" he burst out. "We're going to have so much power we can rule the whole world!"

"Timothy!" Millicent scolded him. "You know Grant told you not to talk about that."

Stockton smiled. "It's all right now, Millicent. It's too late for anyone to stop us. Poor Marshal Long here has no power over us."

"I got the power of the United States Justice Department backing me up," Longarm warned.

Stockton laughed and said, "I'm sorry, Marshal, but human governments are puny compared to the power that I'll wield before this night is over."

"Power that should have been mine," Thorne rumbled.

"Don't get ambitious and ruin everything now, Lucius," Stockton warned him. "Do you have the book?"

Thorne nodded. "Everything is ready. The altar has been prepared, in a clearing in the trees not far from here."

"All right. We should get started then." Stockton took Angela's arm. "Come along, my dear. It's time for you to meet your destiny."

"Grant," Marie said in a ragged voice, "what are you going to do?"

"What are we going to do?" Stockton repeated with a smile. "Why, my dear sister, it's simple. With the help of Angela, and with the spells contained in the book that Lucius's men obtained in Paris, we're going to summon the most powerful demon from the netherworld, a demon that will serve us and make our wishes come true and grant us dominion over this world of mortals."

Longarm had heard enough. Grant Stockton was purr-dee crazy. Nobody could call up demons from Hell. But crazy or not, Stockton and his friends were dangerous and had to be stopped. Longarm reached for his gun.

Count von Steglitz stepped up and aimed a slashing blow with his walking stick at Longarm's head. Longarm twisted and managed to take the strike on his shoulder, but the impact numbed his arm. He tried to reach the Colt with his left hand. Jason Lawlor pulled a gun from under his coat and slammed the barrel against Longarm's head. The big lawman staggered, vaguely aware that Marie was screaming and there was other commotion in the room.

Timothy Ford said, "I'm sorry, Marshal. I really did like you." He threw a punch with his uninjured arm. His fist crashed into Longarm's jaw. Longarm dropped to a knee, shook his head to try to clear away the cobwebs that threatened to choke his brain.

"Hit him again, Timothy," Millicent urged.

"No, that's enough," Stockton said. He stepped forward and plucked Longarm's revolver from its holster. "Marshal Long can't harm us now."

"Grant, you're insane," Marie said. "You can't mean what you said. Please, tell me it's all some . . . some terrible joke. . . ."

Stockton shook his head. "I'm sorry, Marie, but it's very real. We've all studied the ritual, and we know it will work. Nothing can stop us . . . and now that you know the truth, I want you to be part of it, too. You're my sister, and I love you. I want you to rule the world at my side."

"No!" Marie screamed. "No!" She bolted toward the door.

The corpselike vaquero Ramón loomed up in front of her. He grabbed her arms, leering at her.

"Don't harm her!" Lucius Thorne snapped. "Just see that she stays here, where she can't interfere."

"Sí, patrón." Ramón husked. "And the gringo lawman?"

"Wait until we're gone," Thorne ordered, "and then kill him."

Lawlor struck again, smashing the barrel of his pistol against Longarm's head. Longarm pitched forward onto his face, landing in a pool of inky blackness that swallowed him whole.

# Chapter 29

Longarm was unconscious only for a moment, as his iron constitution asserted itself and his will dragged him back from the blackness. But he kept his eyes closed and lay motionless on the carpeted floor as he listened to the others filing out of the room. He heard Stockton say, "Jason, bring my sister along, will you?"

Marie struggled—Longarm heard the sounds of it—but she was no match for Lawlor. He dragged her out of the parlor.

Longarm's mind struggled to grasp everything that had happened here tonight. He had known all along that Stockton was up to something no good, but he never would have believed that the man was some sort of crazy devil worshipper. Longarm had heard of such things but never encountered them. His was a world of bank robbers, rustlers, and assorted owlhoots and bandidos. What he had heard tonight was a manifestation of a darker, more sinister evil, the sort of evil that sprang from a deluded, diseased mind.

Unfortunately, there seemed to be plenty of those to go around. . . .

He heard the gravelly chuckle that came from Ramón's

throat, and a second later, the metallic ratcheting of a gun being cocked.

Longarm moved.

Ramón had expected to shoot an unconscious man in the back of the head. Instead, Longarm flung himself into a roll as the vaquero's gun roared. As he came over onto his back Longarm lashed out with his right leg, slamming the heel of his boot into Ramón's knee. Ramón cried out in pain and stumbled forward, just in time to catch the toe of Longarm's other boot in his balls. He dropped his gun, clapped both hands to his injured privates, and doubled over. Longarm came up off the floor swinging a round-house punch that slammed into Ramón's jaw and sent the vaquero crashing down and out.

Longarm had just scooped up the gun Ramón had dropped when the door into the parlor burst open. Spinning around, Longarm leveled the weapon, but his finger froze on the trigger when he realized he was staring over the barrel at Pierre Dushane.

"Marshal Long!" Dushane exclaimed. "You are all right?"

"My head hurts a mite where that son of a bitch Lawlor pistol-whipped me, but I'm fine," Longarm said.

"I followed as you said, and as I was slipping up to the house I heard screams."

Longarm nodded grimly. "That was Marie Stockton. She didn't know what her brother had planned for tonight, and when she found out she didn't like it."

"And just what does *M'sieur* Stockton have planned?" Dushane asked.

Longarm said, "Him and Thorne and the others are going to call up the Devil from Hades."

The French detective's eyes widened. "Name of a name! When I found out that book they stole in Paris was some sort of sorcerous tome, I feared as much."

"You don't believe all that, do you?"

178

"It matters not what I believe, *mon ami*, but rather what Stockton and his acolytes believe . . . and what they plan to do in an effort to make their mad dreams come true."

"Yeah," Longarm said, "the way I figure it, they plan to kill Angela Boothe in one of them human sacrifices, just like the old Aztecs did down in Mexico."

Dushane nodded. "Murder and the blood of an innocent often play their parts in such rituals."

Angela wasn't all that innocent, Longarm thought, but that didn't matter. From what Stockton had said, Longarm guessed that he and the others planned to kill her, and if Marie didn't settle down and go along with them, her life might be in danger, too.

"Come on," Longarm said. "We've got to stop them."

They paused only long enough to tie Ramón's hands and feet so that he couldn't get free. Then they left the house, which seemed to be empty of other servants, and then trotted out into the orchard that ran for several miles behind the massive structure.

Quietly, Longarm told Dushane, "Thorne said the altar had been prepared somewhere out here. I ain't sure how we'll find it—"

Dushane held up a hand. "Listen."

Longarm heard it, a low, deep sound that after a moment he identified as chanting. He had heard Indians chant something like that during their sacred dances and rituals, but the murmur that came through the air tonight had an eerie quality that made the hair stand up on the back of Longarm's neck. Pure evil, he thought again.

He and Dushane began making their way through the orchard, guided by the chants of madmen.

After a few minutes Longarm spotted a fire up ahead. He and Dushane catfooted toward the flames, and as they approached they slowed down before they ventured into the circle of light cast by the fire. They had a pretty good

179

view through the trees, and what they saw made Longarm's blood run cold.

What looked like a single solid chunk of gleaming black stone had been hauled in and put down in the middle of a small clearing. A large bonfire had been built on the other side of the black stone so that it cast its garish glare over the altar. People in hooded black robes stood around the stone, and between them Longarm caught a glimpse of pale, bare flesh. A couple of the lunatics shifted, and then Longarm could see Angela Boothe lying there on the black stone, naked as the day she was born, with bonds around her wrists and ankles that were fastened to the ground on either side of the altar so that she was splayed out obscenely. One of the hooded figures moved up beside her . . .

The figure used one hand to throw back the hood of its robe while the other lifted a knife with a large, gleaming blade. Longarm's jaw tightened when he saw what was under the hood. The figure didn't have the head of a man at all, but rather the head of a goat, complete with curving horns. He spoke in a loud voice, in a forgotten tongue that was like nothing Longarm had heard before. Something about the words made them sound as if human mouths shouldn't even be able to pronounce them. The other figures around the altar chanted the blasphemies back to the goat-headed man.

Of course, the fella didn't really have the head of a goat. It was a mask, Longarm told himself. And under that mask was Grant Stockton. Longarm recognized his voice.

Off to one side, Marie was on her knees, sobbing. One of the hooded figures stood over her, guarding her. Clearly, she wasn't going to go along with her brother's madness. In a way, Longarm was glad to see that, but it also put Marie in more danger.

"Seen enough?" he whispered to Dushane.

*"Certainement,"* the Frenchman whispered. He raised his gun.

So did Longarm, but he paused as Stockton's voice rose even more. He was getting to the end of the ritual now, Longarm sensed, and he raised the knife higher above Angela. She didn't struggle, didn't even really seem to know what was going on. Stockton must have given her more of the drug to ensure her willing cooperation in her own murder. The knife poised, ready to strike.

Something moved in the flames.

Longarm saw it for an instant, but then he fired, the Colt roaring and bucking in his hand as he squeezed off a shot. The bullet struck Stockton's wrist, shattering it and sending the knife spinning off into the fire. A bright flash, almost like lightning, seared the darkness, blinding Longarm for a second. But his eyes recovered quickly, and he rushed forward.

The others threw their hoods back. Features that should have been normal were twisted by madness into something barely recognizable. Jason Lawlor jerked a gun from under his robe and swung the barrel toward Marie, ready to blow her brains out. Dushane fired first, his pistol cracking as he sent a slug into Lawlor's body. Lawlor staggered and dropped to his knees, crying, "No! No, it can't be!"

But it was, and he pitched forward onto his face.

Count von Steglitz roared a curse and charged at Longarm, swinging his walking stick like a club. The Prussian's movements were awkward because of his wounded leg. Longarm shot the other leg out from under him and didn't feel a bit bad about it.

"Stop them!" Millicent Ford screamed at her husband. "They're going to ruin everything!"

Timothy swung around and moved to block Longarm from the altar. Longarm held his fire. He liked Timothy, despite everything, and figured that the none-too-bright young man had been led into this madness by his shrew of a wife. "Get your hands up and back off, Tim," Longarm warned him.

"I'm sorry, Marshal. I can't do that." He lunged at Longarm.

Longarm met that charge with a looping left fist that crashed into Timothy's jaw. The young man went down, tried to get up, slipped back onto the ground. He was stunned and out of the fight. Dushane was covering Edward and Claire Wilcox, who looked more frightened and confused than dangerous.

That left Stockton.

He had fallen when Longarm shot him, but now he staggered back to his feet, ripped the goat mask off his head, and lunged toward the altar. His right wrist was broken, but his left hand was all right, and he grabbed Angela by the throat and started squeezing. "Die!" he shouted. "You have to die! You were promised to the Unholy One as his bride. . . ."

Crazy as a loon, Longarm thought as he drew a bead.

Before he could fire, Marie leaped at her brother and tried to tear his strangling hand away from Angela's throat. "No, Grant!" she cried. "Stop it! For God's sake, leave her alone!"

Stockton threw back his head and cackled a laugh. "No, not for God's sake! God has no place here!"

Marie gave him one more shove, putting all her strength into it. That was enough to break Stockton's grip on Angela. He stumbled backward toward the fire, and as Longarm watched, the flames seemed to reach out like a giant hand and wrap blazing fingers around Stockton. The robe Stockton wore had gotten into the fire, and now it was burning, burning with a fierceness that enveloped Stockton's whole body in a matter of a heartbeat. Stockton screamed. He whirled around and around as Marie shrank back from him in horror, and when he finally came to a stop facing the fire, he shrieked, "No! Come back! Don't desert me now!"

And then he threw himself even deeper into the flames, collapsing as sparks showered up and cast a glow high in the sky.

Longarm reached Marie's side and put an arm around her shoulders, drawing her away from the awful sight of her brother burning to death. Dushane had produced a clasp knife from his pocket and was using it to cut the bonds holding Angela to the altar. When she was free, she rolled limply off the black stone and fell to the ground on the far side, away from the flames. She was senseless from the drugs, but they would wear off in time. How she dealt with the aftermath of what had almost happened to her was her own problem, Longarm thought.

He was more worried about how he was going to explain all this to Billy Vail.

# Chapter 30

Lucius Thorne was gone, along with the vaqueros who worked for him. Even Ramón had been freed and taken with them. Longarm and Dushane hadn't noticed when Thorne slipped away from the fracas. Dushane still wanted to arrest him for the murder of the old man in Paris, the old man from whom the book containing the unholy ritual had been stolen, and the French detective planned to continue his pursuit.

When they searched the house, they didn't find the book, either. That made Longarm a mite uneasy, but he figured Thorne was going to be too busy trying to avoid the law to get up to too much mischief. Anyway, all those spells and suchlike weren't real. Longarm was hardheaded enough to know that.

Jason Lawlor was dead, and so was Grant Stockton. The others were all in custody, although Longarm wasn't quite sure what they would be charged with. They had known that Stockton planned to kill Angela Boothe and had gone along with it. That was enough for a start. Although considering the fact that all of them were rich, they probably wouldn't wind up behind bars.

Longarm spent a week in Los Angeles with Marie,

ignoring the telegrams Billy Vail sent him urging him to get back to Denver and try to explain this mess in person. She was pretty shaken by everything that had happened and spent a lot of time just staring off into space. Longarm talked to her, quietly and calmly, about everything and nothing, and slowly she came back from wherever she had gone. Finally, they made love one night, and when it was over he held her as she cried, and when she spoke there was renewed strength in her voice to go with the pain.

"I'm sorry. I never knew what he had planned. I can't believe it, even now. But . . . he was my brother. I loved him. I didn't know he was . . . insane."

Longarm stroked her hair and said, "I know you didn't. I reckon with some folks it's sort of like walking along a cliff. You're fine as long as you watch where you're going, but if you're not careful you can fall off . . . and it's a long way down."

She nodded, her cheek wet with tears where it rested against his broad chest. "None of it was real," she whispered. "It was all madness."

"Yep," Longarm said.

But he didn't tell her that for a moment, as those flames had leaped so high, he had seemed to see a giant, laughing face in them, and that when Grant Stockton had plunged into the fire, he had been leaping right into that gaping mouth. . . .

Nope, he never told her that at all, nor anyone else, neither.

Watch for

**LONGARM AND THE TWO-BIT POSSE**

the 312<sup>th</sup> novel in the exciting LONGARM
series from Jove

*Coming in November!*

## Explore the exciting Old West with one of the men who made it wild!

# LONGARM

## GIANT-SIZED ADVENTURE FROM AVENGING ANGEL LONGARM.

---

## LONGARM AND THE DEADLY DEAD MAN
### 0-515-13547-X

## LONGARM AND THE BARTERED BRIDES
### 0-515-13834-7